Retur

Return to the Wells is the sev

Series. It follows the fortu

and Sebastian (and their ba

trouble over her engagem

Rosetti, ballerina.

It looks as if everything is 'set fair' for Ella – her dancing is supremely beautiful; her place in the Sadler's Wells ballet company is assured. But there are many pitfalls in the path of a ballerina, and, in Ella's case, it is her health. She is a delicate girl, and illness claims her. After a year in Switzerland, however, she comes into her own, and even dances before royalty in the Théâtre National of Lausanne.

Also by Lorna Hill in Piccolo

Lorna Hill

Return to
The Wells

Piccolo Books

To all at 'Treetops' with love

First published 1955 by Evans Brothers Ltd
This Piccolo edition published 1985 by Pan Books Ltd,
Cavaye Place, London SW10 9PG
9 8 7 6 5 4 3 2 1
© Lorna Hill 1955
ISBN 0 330 28715 X
Photoset by Parker Typesetting Service, Leicester
Printed and bound in Great Britain by
Hunt Barnard Printing, Aylesbury, Bucks

Contents

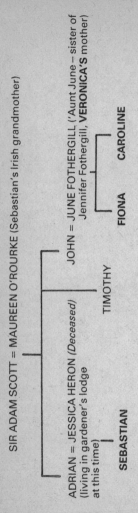

SCOTT FAMILY TREE

SIR ADAM SCOTT = MAUREEN O'ROURKE (Sebastian's Irish grandmother)

ADRIAN = JESSICA HERON *(Deceased)*
(living in gardener's lodge at this time)

TIMOTHY

JOHN = JUNE FOTHERGILL ('Aunt June – sister of Jennifer Fothergill, **VERONICA'S** mother)

SEBASTIAN

FIONA   **CAROLINE**

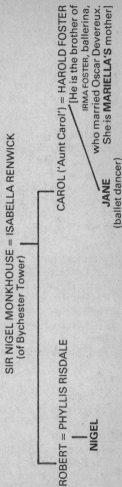

MONKHOUSE FAMILY TREE

SIR NIGEL MONKHOUSE = ISABELLA RENWICK
(of Bychester Tower)

ROBERT = PHYLLIS RISDALE

NIGEL

CAROL ('Aunt Carol') = HAROLD FOSTER
[He is the brother of IRMA FOSTER, ballerina, who married Oscar Devereux. She is **MARIELLA'S** mother]

JANE
(ballet dancer)

Part One

Chapter 1

Timothy

Blackheath Vicarage was actually two pit cottages knocked into one. In front of the house was a strip of garden planted with laurel bushes, because they were the only things that would grow in Blackheath, owing to the fumes that came from the colliery across the way. Guarding the laurel bushes (just in case anybody wanted to uproot them and carry them off in the night) was a strip of iron railings, much beloved by the local youth who rattled their sticks upon it as they passed, but much hated by the vicar because, when he was in a hurry, he had to go all the way round by the drive. Timothy, the vicar's nineteen-year-old son, was in the habit of taking the railings in his stride (literally), sometimes at the expense of his trousers. The 'drive' was a strip of concrete that wound in desultory fashion from the rickety gate up to the front door. The parish council had clubbed together and laid down the drive some years ago so that it would be easy for the vicar to 'keep'. Mrs Roebottom, the vicar's wife, never ceased to wonder at the way in which the frail weeds burst through the cement and bloomed notwithstanding. They were indeed an object lesson, thought Cynthia Roebottom. She hadn't the heart to uproot them.

Branching off from the drive was a smaller path, unashamedly weedy, which led to a door in the wall jutting out at right angles to the vicarage proper. On the far side of this door, decently hidden from the common gaze, was the yard. This square space had a brick floor with coarse grass sprouting from the cracks, and it had a distinct 'rake', like a provincial stage, owing to colliery workings underneath. There was a large, ominous crack across the middle of it, but, as yet, the earth hadn't opened and no one had dropped through! A large ash-pit dominated the yard, but Mrs Roebottom used it as a receptacle for old tins and bottles. Ashes were too precious to be thrown away. They were used to bank up the fire in the vicar's study at nights.

At the moment when our story begins, the yard was occupied by Timothy Roebottom's motor car. From underneath the vehicle came the sound of cheerful whistling:

> 'Good Christian men re-joi-oi-oice
> With heart, and soul and voi-oi-oice—!'

Last night Timothy had attended the carol service at his father's church, and his vocal repertoire had been influenced thereby. His long legs, clad in corduroy trousers so old that their colour was nondescript, stuck out from between the two back wheels of the car, and the foot of one of them tapped the frozen ground in time with the stirring tune.

> 'Give ye heed to what we say!
> News! News! News!'

sang Timothy. His disposition was sanguine at all times, but today there was a special reason for his cheerfulness. By this morning's post his mother had received a cheque from Messrs Courtney Ltd in payment for her drawings which were to illustrate a book of ballet they were publishing. The cheque was for £300, and never in all her life had Mrs Roebottom had so much money in a piece, to be spent on herself. Yes, the vicar had insisted that it should belong to his wife alone, seeing that it was a windfall, and she had earned it.

8

Having cashed a cheque and received a large bundle of notes which she stuffed into her shabby brown leather handbag, Mrs Roebottom set off to make her purchases. She felt rather as if she had robbed a bank or was running off with the proceeds of the parish sale of work! Walking like a cat on hot bricks, because of the slipperiness of the road, she reached her first objective – the department stores, where she bought a new overcoat for her husband. She had to guess the size, because she would never have persuaded him to let her spend so much money. 'Never mind,' thought Mrs Roebottom, 'it'll be warm, even if it doesn't fit like Savile Row!'

She went from the gents' outfitting to the gents' underwear, and bought Mr Roebottom three flannel shirts, two pairs of pyjamas, several pairs of socks, a pair of slippers, and a dressing-gown. He had never had a dressing-gown since he'd left college, but had always 'made do' with an old coat. When she came out of the store, she had spent just half her earnings.

Next came a visit to the grocery department, where she chose the largest and juiciest piece of beef to roast. They would have a celebration that evening after the jumble sale was over. Roast beef, chipped potatoes, a trifle (because Timothy loved it), blue-veined cheese, her husband's favourite, and coffee and chocolate biscuits to follow.

Having finished her shopping, Cynthia took her parcels home, and astonished Timothy by pressing several of the remaining notes into his hand.

'But Mother—' protested the young man. Fifty quid! Gosh! You don't really mean it? You can't spare all that.'

'Yes, I can, dear,' said Mrs Roebottom. 'Your father wouldn't take a penny. He insisted that I should spend it all on myself.' She didn't notice that there was anything contradictory about her action or her words, and neither did Timothy. He was overcome, all the same.

9

'But Mother – you're really sure? Why, I could paint the whole bus for that – not only the wheels. And I could have her re-treaded all round, not only the back ones. And I could buy a fog-lamp—'

'Run along then and buy one, dear,' said Cynthia Roebottom to her curly-haired, six-foot son, 'if that will make you happy.'

'Happy!' exclaimed the overcome youth. 'Happy! Oh, boy!'

We now know the reason for the whistling – the large tin of scarlet paint that stood beside the garage door (enough to paint the whole bus), and a new and shining fog-lamp that protruded aggressively from the front of the tiny car like a wart on the nose of a wart-hog.

Timothy had poured some of the red paint out of the large can into a smaller one, and was at that moment engaged in painting the parts of the chassis that showed. He wanted to be very smart these days because he had met A Girl. He thought of her in capital letters, because she was different from any other girl he had met. He didn't often think of girls – he was too busy. (There were so many other things to think about.) But this particular girl had occupied his thoughts for quite a lot of the forty-eight hours that had elapsed since he had met her at Charlton's wedding over at Bychester. For one thing, she had disappeared on the stroke of twelve, like her namesake Cinderella, and so far he hadn't been able to find out her second name. Everyone knew her as just 'Ella'. It was very intriguing, and enough to set one wondering. Oh, well, thought Timothy, carefully painting the insides of the spokes of the back wheels, it was only a question of time. He'd find out! . . . Must have the old bus smart in case she came back for another holiday, as she no doubt would, since she was a friend of the Eliots.

'Sing, choirs of angels!' sang Timothy, breaking out into the melody in the tenor.

'Sing in exultation!
Sing, all ye citizens of Heaven above!'

Yes, he felt like singing, despite the fact that it was exceedingly cold lying on his back on a bit of sacking underneath the car. This afternoon he was meeting old Dicky Lister, and the two of them were going to join a lot of other chaps – members of the King's College rock climbing club – and they were going to have a day on Simonside. Ought to be super in the snow! Afterwards he would call at Bracken Hall and find out The Girl's name. Veronica Weston would know it. Then he'd write to her and tell her how much he had liked her dancing. Luckily Timothy did not know that his plans would come to naught, since both Veronica and her husband had flown back to London by the evening plane last night.

'Good Christian men re-joi-oi-oice!' he sang, returning to his first carol. 'With heart and soul and voi-oi-oice!'

Once more Ella's face came to his mind. Pretty? Good lord, no! He supposed some people might think she was positively plain. Yet, could you call a person plain who had large dark eyes, and a sweet, shy smile, and was moreover as dainty and as full of grace as a fairy? To Timothy she was neither pretty nor plain. She was just 'Ella', the most attractive girl he had met so far.

'Timothy!' came Mrs Roebottom's voice from the house. 'Lunch is ready, dear.'

'OK, Mother,' answered Timothy. 'Just coming!'

Still whistling (he had changed to 'Good King Wenceslas' by this time), he wriggled out from underneath the car, and stood for a moment proudly contemplating the vehicle. Then his gaze left it and fell upon the ramshackle house, with its lopsided windows and badly fitting doors.

'House could do with a spot of paint, too,' he murmured. 'Could give the jolly old door a coat anyway.' He measured the amount of scarlet paint left in the large can with a

11

practised eye. 'Enough left for that.' He slung the can into the garage and shut the door with a clang, adding under his breath, 'Do it tomorrow.'

'*Timothy!*'

'Coming, Mother.'

He wiped his hands on a rag, and then on his corduroy trousers. After which, he swung across the yard with a graceful stride and pushed open the back door. An appetising smell met him. Wiping his shoes carefully on the neatly folded sack that did duty for a door-mat (no need to take dirt into the house for his mother to clean up), he washed his hands under the kitchen tap, ran a pocket-comb through his shock of curly fair hair, and went into the front part of the house. On the way he met his mother carrying in the soup on a tray. He took it from her without a word and deposited the tray on the dumb-waiter in the dining-room. Then he placed the soup plates round the table with a practised hand. Wait at table? Why, yes, of course Timothy Roebottom could wait at table. He could do other things too. Wash the dishes, for instance, and without breaking any of them. Wash the kitchen floor as well. Did it most weeks. He'd even tackled the family washing when Mrs Carter, who charred for the Roebottoms two days a week, was away, and done it without a washing machine too! Once he and his father had cooked the Christmas dinner (which was on Boxing Day at the vicarage for obvious reasons) when his mother was in hospital, and made not such a bad fist at it either. Timothy was what is known as 'domesticated', and not ashamed of it either.

Mrs Roebottom looked at her tall, curly-headed son across the dining table, and her heart overflowed with love for him. He had such a sunny nature. It didn't matter what went wrong (and goodness knows there were plenty of ups and downs in the poverty-stricken vicarage), Timothy always met the situation with: 'Oh, well, it might be worse,'

12

or: 'Never mind, Mother, it'll come out in the wash!' At the moment, however, the vicarage sky was without a cloud. The vicar was wearing his new shirt and slippers, and she had bought a new dress for herself. She had even bought sweets for the Sunday school children so they might share in her good fortune. The rest of the money was safely deposited in the bank ready for a rainy day.

'You realise that this may happen again, Cynthia,' said Mr Roebottom, passing up his plate for another helping of soup.

'What may happen again, dear?' said the vicar's wife, her mind flying like a bird from the recent carol service to the parish social next week, and finally coming to rest on the jumble sale this evening. 'You mean the bother about the tables? Well, I hope not, Matthew, because we shall need several more for the social, and if there's all this fuss about getting the two long ones—'

'No, no, no!' exclaimed the vicar. 'I wasn't talking about tables. I was talking about your drawings. This may be just the beginning. You may get more commissions.'

Mrs Roebottom's very blue eyes opened wide, and her thin cheeks flushed.

'Oh, I shouldn't think so. Courtneys have been very kind, of course, but—'

'Kind my foot!' exploded the vicar. 'You don't think that Courtneys are a charitable institution, do you, my dear, existing solely for the laudable purpose of helping the penniless wives of the clergy? Not a bit of it! Your drawings are good, and they know it. They'll be a success. I expect you'll end up a rich woman, and I shall be known as "the husband of the famous Cynthia Roebottom!" '

'You do like romancing, don't you! said Cynthia, smiling across at her husband, and thinking how very alike he and Timothy were. But in the years to come Mr Roebottom was proved right. Cynthia Roebottom's lovely drawings of the ballet were in great demand, and if she didn't end up by being rich – well, she certainly became comfortably well off.

Now the odd thing is that neither Cynthia nor her husband had happened to refer to little Ella Sordy in Timothy's hearing. Not that they hadn't talked about her. In fact they had talked about little else. They had never tired of saying how strange it was that one small girl coming from a family like the Sordys of Pit Street should have had this influence on the vicarage. It certainly looked as if she was going to change the lives of the Roebottoms altogether! They'd discussed the matter so much between themselves that they imagined Timothy, who had been up at Cambridge at the time, knew all about it, whereas in actual fact he had never so much as heard the name 'Ella' mentioned, or if he had, it hadn't meant anything to him.

'And talking of jumble sales,' put in Cynthia, passing back the vicar's plate, 'you won't forget about it to-night, Timothy dear, will you? You did promise—'

'To fetch and carry!' laughed Timothy. 'OK, Mother, I'll be there. Want any stuff carted across to the hall before I go?'

'Please, dear – if you have the time. I don't want to make you late, though.'

'I'll manage,' said Timothy. He got up, swept the dirty dishes off the table and out into the kitchen, shrugged on his coat – an ex-army duffle-coat with a hood (he never wore the latter over his head, however cold the weather), and went off in search of the 'jumble'. There was a huge pile of it in the back porch and it took Timothy several journeys to and fro to get it all across to the hall. None of it belonged to the Roebottoms themselves. Their clothing, when discarded, was far too old even for the parish jumble sale. It was only fit to be used for floorcloths, and (after being washed) to make the famous Durham miners' 'clippie' mats.

'Well, here's a treat for somebody!' exclaimed Timothy,

14

depositing a large straw hat, with a drooping feather on one side, on the nearest table. 'And what price a fur coat made of genuine – now, what shall we say? – wolf, perhaps!' This strange garment, which resembled nothing so much as a very shaggy door-mat, he gave the place of honour in the middle of the table. All the rest of the stuff he spread out as tastefully as possible – old shoes at one end, undergarments at the other, with a medley of ancient coats, washed-out print dresses, jumpers and cardigans filling in the vast empty space in the middle. Having done this, he gave his work a parting nod of approval, shut and locked the door – 'just in case anybody commits a burglary,' he thought with a grin, 'I *don't* think!' – and dropped the key in at the vicarage. After which he slung on his rucksack, and set off to catch his bus.

Chapter 2

The Jumble Sale

All the world (the Blackheath world, anyway) loves a jumble sale. The whole parish came, and even if they had plenty of money to buy things new out of the shops, they still weren't above getting a bargain at the 'jumble'. It was the gambling instinct, decided Timothy. You bought a bundle of old curtains, and never knew till you got them home whether or not the worn or faded places could be cut out, when you made them into a cover for the settee.

Timothy was as good as his word and arrived on the scene just as the doors opened. Not that he was really needed until the end, when his work was to pack up all the unsold stuff, convey it across to the vicarage in his car, and take it into Newcastle next day to a second-hand clothes dealer, but he knew that his mother liked his presence as moral support. As the people surged into the hall, he couldn't help likening the jumble sale to a rugger scrum. 'Except the finish,' he amended. 'That rather fizzles out like a damp squib . . . Gosh! Look at old Mam Sordy! She's out to get what she wants and no mistake!'

The Sordy family were very much in evidence. Mrs Sordy (known locally as Me Mam) and the two Sordy children (Lily and D'reen) were forcing their way towards the nearest table with the power and attack of a triple battering-ram.

'What a spectacle!' thought Timothy. 'Mam Sordy, with a face like a newly baked brick, and those two fat, bold-eyed, giggling kids!' His attention was called away for a moment by his mother, who wanted him to try on a coat and waistcoat for a prospective customer.

'M-m, quite natty!' said the customer, a Mrs Duffy who lived near the Sordys and who prided herself on 'cutting down' and 'making over' old clothes. 'Turn round, Timothy, love, and let's see the back. A bit ower big, but I could mak' it over for our Jimmy. Aye, a'll tak' it, Mrs Roebottom. Fifty pence, yer said?' The coins clinked into the milk basin that stood at Cynthia's right hand, the clothes were bundled up and stuffed into Mrs Duffy's capacious bag, and the next customer pressed forward.

Timothy's attention was once more caught, and held, by Mam Sordy, who was having a heated argument with a member of the parochial church council, a Mrs Strong. This lady, by virtue of her office, was on the other side of the counter, helping to sell the jumbles.

'It ain't no use you tellin' me you didna tak' it,' Mrs Sordy was saying at the top of her voice, 'for I seed you wi' me own eyes. A right down nice pinny – never a thing wrong wi't, except one o' the strings missing. Yes,' she added to the interested spectators, 'she put it in her bag before ever the doors were opened. I seed her through the key-hole . . . oh, yes, she did . . . I tell you she did . . .'

Poor Mrs Strong, who, belying her name, was unusually timid, positively cowered before Mrs Sordy's accusing eye.

'*And* I don't suppose she paid a penny for't,' added Mam Sordy for the benefit of her neighbours. 'Not a penny.'

'Oh, but I did, Mrs Sordy, indeed I did,' said poor Mrs Strong. 'You're wrong about that. I paid twenty pence for it. Didn't I, Mrs Roebottom?'

'Ah, so you *did* tak' it?' Mam Sordy pounced like a cat on a mouse. 'I knew't!'

'Just a moment,' put in Cynthia Roebottom quietly (not for the first time Timothy marvelled at the way in which his mother, quiet and gentle though she was, managed to

17

restore order). 'At the last council meeting a resolution was passed to the effect that any helper at the jumble sale could buy one article before the doors were opened. The pinafore happened to be Mrs Strong's choice. She paid twenty pence for it; I saw her put it into the bowl myself.'

For a moment Mrs Sordy was silent, the wind taken out of her sails, but not for long.

'So that's the way o't!' she burst out. 'Well, if all the best goods are to be took aforehand by the church council, this is the last jumble sale *I'll* be coming to. You can put that in your pipe and smoke it!'

'Only *one* garment each, Mrs Sordy,' repeated Cynthia.

'Only plenty!' retorted Me Mam, determined to have the last word on the subject. 'Oh, well, now I'm here, give us them two shirts. They'll do for our Dad. Five pee apiece, OK.' Ten pence clattered into the basin, and the shirts disappeared into Me Mam's ever-open bag, and she elbowed her way on to the next table, leaving the helpers heaving vast sighs of relief at her going. Mam Sordy, it will be gathered, was not a popular character.

Timothy stood by the door watching the proceedings curiously. 'One day,' he said to himself, 'I'll write a book about all this! Golly, look at old Mrs Witherspoon nibbling on the edge of the crowd like a timid little mouse at a piece of cheese!' As a matter of fact, old Mrs Witherspoon was remarkably successful at her nibbling, and managed to buy up quite a small wardrobe of shrunken garments that nobody else could wear. She herself had shrunk considerably with the passing of time, and now looked, as Timothy had said, like a little grey mouse.

A jumble sale never lasts very long, and the Blackheath sale was nearly over when Timothy's gaze came back to the Sordy family. Me Mam was sitting on the steps leading to the cloakroom, her feet apart, and between them the ancient shopping-bag, distended into a grotesque shape by the number and variety of her purchases. Lily was trying on the unbought hats and giggling loudly, whilst D'reen was reading the evening paper that someone had brought in and flung down on the end of the now almost empty table.

'Oo! look at this'n!' cried Lily. 'Smasher, eh?' She had snatched a handful of crumpled grey net and satin from the small heap of unsold garments, and was holding it up against herself. 'What price me dance dress?'

For a fleeting moment the grey net struck a chord in Timothy's memory. A grey and white ballet dress! He remembered buying the material for little Miss Jones to make such a one for that poor, plain little what's-her-name (he had never heard her name in actual fact). He wondered what had become of the kid.

'Mother!' he called, determined to find out. But Cynthia was busy counting out a pile of copper and silver into a customer's hand in exchange for a one pound note, and she didn't hear him. The next moment someone claimed Timothy's attention, and the opportunity was lost. Had he but known it, the net dress was that very same ballet dress – the dress that had altered little Ella Sordy's whole life (and incidentally Mrs Roebottom's too). When she had left Pit Street, she had wrapped it up and put it away in the cupboard she shared with Lily and D'reen, not knowing that she had said goodbye to Pit Street for ever. Her Mam had promised to keep if for her, but Mam Sordy's promises were like piecrust, made to be broken when it suited her. So, when the 'church lady' came round begging for jumble, the grey and white dress was the first to be thrown out.

'No use keepin' rubbish,' said Me Mam. 'T'won't fit our Lily or our D'reen, and our Ella'll never miss it.'

Unknown to Timothy, his mother saw the sad, crushed little ballet dress when she was packing away the unsold 'jumbles.' It was priced five pence, so she bought it, and took it home with her without saying a word to anyone (they

19

might accuse her of being sentimental). She didn't know, of course, that Timothy had bought the material for it in the first place, but she remembered that Ella Sordy had worn it in Mary Martin's summer show. She felt she owed a debt to Ella Sordy, though some people might have said that Ella Sordy owed a debt to Mrs Roebottom. She certainly didn't guess that she was saving the dress for posterity; that generations of dancers to come would stare at the glass case containing the very first ballet dress worn by the great *ballerina*, Ella Rosetti.

The jumble sale was finished at last, the tables had been cleared, the people had gone home. Lily and D'reen were two of the last to go, and they had left their paper spreadeagled on the floor. Timothy picked it up out of sheer force of habit, and was about to throw it into the fireplace, when his eye caught a picture on the front page. Under the picture was an announcement:

'A marriage has been arranged and will shortly take place,' read Timothy, 'between Nigel, only son of Sir Robert Monkhouse, Bt., and Lady Monkhouse of Bychester Tower, Northumberland, and Mariella, only daughter of Mr and Mrs Oscar Deveraux (Irma Foster), 140a Fortnum Mansions, W1. Miss Foster is the niece of Mr and Mrs Foster of Monks Hollow, Northumberland.' The laughing face of Mariella looked back at him as he stood holding the newspaper.

'Well!' thought Timothy. 'And I imagined the girl was keen on Campbell of Inveross! She danced with him nearly all night at Charlton's wedding, anyway. It just goes to show you never know where you are with girls!'

With which profound observation Timothy screwed the paper up into a ball, then, on second thought, unscrewed it again (perhaps his mother might be interested) and put it into his pocket. In so doing, his fingers came into contact with a small, smooth object. He drew it out slowly. It was a pink satin ballet shoe.

'I wonder who she is, and where she lives?' he said to himself. He had called at Bracken Hall that afternoon, only to find that Veronica and her husband had already flown back to London, so he hadn't been able to find out anything about his Cinderella. Had he but known it, almost any one of these people at the jumble sale could have told him all he wished to know.

Chapter 3

After the Wedding

Mariella slept late the day after Jane's wedding. The sun was streaming into her room when she woke, and for a few moments she lay there, peacefully watching the light from the snowy garden reflected on the ceiling. Then she sat up . . . Something had happened last night after the dance . . . Nigel . . . he'd asked her to marry him, and she'd refused! Yes, she'd actually said 'no' to the question she'd been praying and praying he would ask her for the last twelve months at least. Life is a funny thing, thought Mariella. One thinks one knows exctly what one wants, and then suddenly one finds one doesn't want it at all. Fickle? Changeable? Nigel, no doubt, would call her these things. But it wasn't true. There was nothing fickle or changeable about Mariella. The truth was that Nigel, with his charm, had drawn a veil over her eyes. Last night the veil had been torn away and she had really seen him for the first time. The episode of the kitten had been the immediate cause of her disillusionment, but the real cause was his inconsiderate, selfish, sometimes downright cruel, behaviour, spread over many months (one might almost say years) – in fact, ever since she had come to Monks Hollow, all that long time ago.

'I wonder how the poor little kitten is?' she thought. 'I must ring up Robin and find out.' The thought of Robin Campbell brought a warm glow to her sore heart. He'd been so kind to her last night when he had opened his door and drawn her into his warm surgery. He'd made her a cup of coffee, and talked soothingly, while he set the kitten's leg.

22

He hadn't asked awkward questions, but had calmly and efficiently gone about his work, thus giving her time to recover her composure. He had called her 'my dear', remembered Mariella, a tinge of pink coming into her cheeks. Of course, that meant nothing; it was quite a common expression nowadays, but it was nice to hear him *say* it, nevertheless. When he had settled the kitten in a blanket-lined box by the stove, he had got out his car again and taken her home, though by this time it was half-past two in the morning, and he had to be up early next day.

What Mariella did not know was that, when Robin had opened his door to her that frosty night and taken her in, he had taken her into his heart also. When he had called her 'my dear', he had meant exactly what he said. Mariella was his 'dear' – dearer to him than anyone else – though whether or not he was dear to her, he knew not. He had yet to find this out. He gathered, however, that something had happened between Mariella and Nigel that night, and he began to hope that perhaps there was a chance for him. He saw, however, how distraught the girl was, and was content to minister to her, and ask no questions for the time being. Patience was a virtue Robin Campbell possessed in a high degree!

After she had finished dressing, Mariella ran down to the little cloakroom in the hall where the telephone was, and picked up the receiver. There was a message written on the pad lying beside the instrument, and, while she dialled Robin's number, she read it. (Evidently Jennie, the maid, had taken it down some time earlier). 'Mr Monkhouse will be calling at about eleven o'clock,' said the message.

Mariella's hand, holding the receiver, shook so much she could hardly answer Robin when she heard his voice at the other end of the wire, asking her how she was, after the excitement of yesterday's wedding.

'Oh, I'm all right – at least, I think I am. The wedding?

23

Oh, of course, I was forgetting about it for the moment – yes, it was lovely, wasn't it? No, there's nothing the matter. I'm just a bit tired. I've just got up' – if this sounded contradictory, Mariella was far too agitated to notice it – 'yes, I'm going for a ride after I've had my breakfast. Goodbye.'

She put down the receiver, and then suddenly realised that she hadn't asked him about the kitten. In fact, she hadn't asked him anything at all! He must have thought she was crazy, ringing him up about nothing! It was all Nigel's fault. She remembered, now, that he had said he would come over for his answer, but she hadn't thought he really meant it. She had said 'no' so very definitely. Surely he must have believed her?

It was obvious that Mariella didn't know Nigel. Any opposition only made him the more determined. Until last night he hadn't made up his mind whether he wanted to marry Mariella or not. Now he knew! He did want to marry her. In fact, he was going to marry her. Let anyone try to stop him! If Mariella thought she was going to give him the go-by in favour of that gaunt, long-legged Robin Campbell, well, she had another thought coming! He would go to any lengths – any lengths. Not for nothing was Nigel the only son of the squire of the tiny feudal village of Bychester, ruled over by his forebears for generations!

Fortunately Mariella had no idea of all this. All she knew was that she mustn't be here when Nigel came. He'd start arguing, and trying to jockey her into saying yes. She couldn't stand that! She poured herself out a cup of coffee, and drank it so quickly she almost choked. Then, after a mouthful of toast ('Nothing else, thank you, Jennie, I'm not very hungry'), she ran quickly upstairs again. She would say goodbye to her mother, who, she knew, was going back to London by the afternoon train, and after this she would go for a long ride and not come back again until the coast was clear.

Irma was dressing when Mariella knocked softly on the door.

'Come in,' she said in her slightly foreign-sounding voice. (Mariella could never decide whether her mother had caught the accent on her travels abroad, or from her husband, Oscar Deveraux, or whether she merely affected it because it sounded romantic.)

'Goodbye, Mummy,' said Mariella, running over to her mother and kissing her. 'It's been lovely to see you, even though it hasn't been for very long. I expect I shall be coming up to town some time soon.' She said this as a mere matter of form, because it wasn't at all likely. Mariella hated London!

'Goodbye, my darling,' said Irma, kissing her daughter back warmly. 'I hope you will.'

Mariella left the bedroom with its litter of expensive dressing cases and its aroma of exotic French perfume and went back along the corridor to her own small room with almost a sigh of relief. Now if you think it's strange for a girl to treat her mother almost as if she were a stranger, just remember that Mariella had only seen Irma for odd half-hours all through her childhood, and even these brief periods were interspersed by long stretches of absence when her famous mother was dancing abroad. Added to this was her five years here at Monks Hollow. No wonder this big country house was more home to her than the luxury flat in London's West End! She changed into her riding clothes at top speed, and flew downstairs again. (Nigel was an early riser, she knew, and she wanted to be well away before he arrived. It would be awful to be caught at the gate!) She went round to the stables, and found her Aunt Carol outside in the stable-yard grooming Nancy, her hunter. She looked up when she heard Mariella approach.

'Hullo, lazybones! You must have been tired after yesterday's festivities!' Mrs Foster was one of those uncomfortable people who always get up early, no matter how late they go to bed or how hectic a time they've had the day before. Neither do they take into account the deadly tiring effect of mental strain on more highly – strung people.

'Yes, I *was* rather tired,' Mariella answered guiltily. 'I thought I'd just go off for a ride to work it off. Don't keep lunch for me, Aunt Carol. I'll get some out. I've said goodbye to Mummy.' She waited breathlessly for her aunt's reply, but all she said was: 'Very well, Mariella. I hope you have a nice ride.' So evidently she hadn't read the message on the telephone-pad.

'Oh, and by the way,' went on Mrs Foster, putting the dandy-brush down on the snowy ground, and taking an envelope out of her breeches' pocket, 'if you're going anywhere near Bychester, you might give this note to Lady Monkhouse. It's about the Women's Institute concert. We can't get the concert party from Coldburn, so it'll have to be the Bridgend Gleemen again, I suppose. I do hope everyone isn't sick of hearing them, but really I can't think of anyone else. I'd be glad to know if Phyllis has any ideas.' Not being over-sensitive herself, Aunt Carol didn't notice Mariella's gasp of dismay. Bychester! The very place of all others she wished most to avoid! Then a sudden thought struck the girl. If Nigel was coming over here to Monks Hollow this morning, particularly to see her, then he'd wait for her some little time. He'd surely have lunch here. So really Bychester would be quite safe. She could just leave the note with a maid, and if, by bad luck, she *did* run into Nigel's mother, well, Aunt Phyllis would know nothing of all this, so it wouldn't really matter.

'All right, Aunt Carol,' she promised good-naturedly. 'I'll see she gets it.'

She saddled up Jasmine Flower as quickly as she could,

26

for it was getting horribly late, rode out of one of the back gates, and away across the open moorland, keeping clear of the country road leading to Bychester up which Nigel would come, thus making a long detour and joining the main road at Wark further on. Once on it, she gave a sigh of relief. Nigel never rode along main roads if he could help it. Neither did she, come to that, but today the circumstances were somewhat unusual.

It was a calm, cold day, with a hint of more snow in the air. A flake or two settled upon Mariella's bright uncovered head, like butterflies on a sunny marigold. There was no traffic at all on the road, main though it was, and Mariella didn't meet a single soul, unless you counted a small mongrel dog, out hunting all by itself. Mariella tried to make friends with it, but, after a wag of its tail, it disappeared. It knew exactly where it was going, and was not to be deflected.

'Lucky little dog!' thought Mariella. 'I wish I were as certain of myself. All I know is that I'm not going to marry Nigel.'

The road had been rather open and bleak up to now, but suddenly it dived through a little fir wood. The trees held out snowy arms across the path, and Mariella, forgetting to duck, brought a shower of snow down upon herself and her horse. The little stream by the roadside was frozen and silent, but where it fell over the rocks, or tumbled down the steep bankside, you could hear it gurgling beneath its icy prison. The distant hills, seen through a gap in the trees, were intensely blue, very remote. It was lovely and peaceful, and gradually Mariella began to feel at peace too. After all, she argued, the affair was ended. She'd refused Nigel, and that was that. When he came for his answer this morning and found her gone, he'd know she had meant what she'd said, and he'd choose another girl. There were plenty of girls, Mariella was well aware, who would jump at

Nigel Monkhouse, son and heir of Sir Robert Monkhouse, the squire of Bychester.

She rode along, deep in her thoughts, and suddenly, without realising it, she found herself outside the Dragon Inn at Bridgend. She led her horse round to the stables, found someone to look after him, and went inside. Just over a year ago she'd had lunch there with Nigel, she remembered with a little pang. Funny, these little pangs! Although she was no longer in love with Nigel, she *had* been in love with an imaginary Nigel, and it was odd to think that he didn't exist, in fact never had existed. It left her with an empty, let-down feeling.

'Oh, well, there's one good thing about it,' she said, common sense coming to her aid, 'I can have what I like to eat. I needn't have raspberries!' (Raspberries, even the tinned ones, had always made her come out in spots, ever since she was a little girl.) 'And I can go home when I like, and not have to sit waiting for Nigel.'

She had the inn to herself. There was nobody staying here, of course, at this time of the year, and there wasn't even a stray motorist, or hiker, having his lunch. Mariella sat at a little table by the window, and the waitress, thinking how daft some people were, choosing the coldest spot in the room, when there was a roaring log fire halfway up the chimney, obligingly brought an electric radiator and placed it beside her.

'Oh, thank you,' Mariella said gratefully. 'I'm so sorry you had all that trouble, especially when there's such a lovely fire, but you see I wanted to look at the view.'

It was indeed a view worth looking at. Snowy hills, with deep blue shadows lying in the hollows; ink-black fir woods, with the brown tracks made by rabbits, pheasants, and other wild creatures, criss-crossing the rides and the fire-lanes; narrow hard white road leading away over the hills to who knew where?

There was no regular lunch, but Mariella, hungry after her scanty breakfast and her ride, tackled the fried ham and eggs, with mince-pies to follow, with a will, and thought what a lovely meal it was. So peaceful and homely! Yet the room was haunted by memories of that other luncheon party a year ago. Everything was the same – the locust in the jar, the bookcase full of encyclopaedias (still locked), the same pampas grass in the same blue vase. Nothing was changed. Only Nigel's voice was absent . . . 'Hullo, Mariella! Still here? Don't say you waited for me . . . Well, now you're here, you can ride Bess home for me . . . Do get a move on, there's a good girl! . . .'

Yes, she'd had a lucky escape. And yet these ghosts, these pathetic little ghosts, kept popping up. She would have to bring Robin here to 'lay' them. Robin had called her 'my dear', and had told her, as he left her on her doorstep at three o'clock in the morning, that if she was ever in any trouble, she was to go to him. She remembered the way he had looked at her when he had said it – as if he was begging for a favour, as if he *wanted* to help her. Robin was not at all handsome, but he was infinitely gentle and kind, and he was moveover, as dependable as the sun in the heavens. He—

'Why!' exclaimed Mariella in amazement. 'I know what's the matter with me! I know why I can't marry Nigel – I'm in love with Robin!'

As she rode home she thought about Robin. It was all very well to know that she had fallen in love with him, but what about his feeling for her? He'd never shown her he thought about her in that way. He'd always been friendly, it's true, but nothing more. So argued Mariella, cautious now.

If Robin Campbell could have heard Mariella arguing thus, he would have been vastly amused, and more than a little puzzled. Surely he couldn't have made it more plain that he adored the very ground Mariella walked on? He

29

hadn't actually *told* her he loved her, it is true, but one can say a thing with one's actions better than putting it into bald words. It never occurred to him that a well-brought-up girl like Mariella couldn't take a thing like that for granted. Until he actually said: 'Mariella, I love you. Will you be my wife?' she couldn't be sure he meant it.

Chapter 4

The Engagement

It was when Mariella saw the sign-post saying BYCHESTER 3 MILES that she remembered with a shock the letter her aunt had given her for Lady Monkhouse. She'd never thought another thing about it until this minute. She glanced at her wrist-watch. Half-past three! If she wasn't quick, Nigel would be back, and she'd run into him, after all. Why, of why, had she dawdled so long, thinking of Robin!

She rode swiftly up the moorland road, and in through the gates of Bychester Tower. The ancient building looked especially menacing, she thought, with its lop-sided pepper-box roof leering down at her, and the dark, still waters of the moat, frozen over and lightly powered with snow. She rode round to one of the side doors (too dangerous to go to the front), hoping she'd be able to leave the note and escape while the going was good. And then, just as she leaned down from the saddle to push the bell, the worst happened.

'Oh, hullo, Mariella,' said a deep voice – Aunt Phyllis's voice. 'We've been expecting you.'

'Expecting me?' echoed Mariella. 'I – I don't understand.'

'Don't be coy, Mariella!' said Lady Monkhouse, slapping her riding-breeches with her crop. 'Surely I have a right to expect a visit from my new daughter-in-law?'

Mariella was so astonished and horrified that for a moment she said nothing. It was then that Nigel himself appeared. He took a couple of purposeful strides towards her, swung her down from the horse's back, and before she knew what he was about, he had taken her in his arms and kissed her.

'*Nigel!*' gasped Mariella in a muffled voice, trying vainly to tear herself free. 'Nigel, let me go at once!'

'Oh, don't mind the mater,' laughed Nigel. 'She's all in favour. Thoroughly approves. In fact, everyone does. Your people were thrilled to the back teeth when I told them the news this morning.'

'The news?' gasped Mariella, freeing herself at last. 'What news?'

'The news of our engagement, of course,' said Nigel.

By this time Lady Monkhouse had retreated tactfully, leaving 'the young people', as she called them, together. Hastily Mariella put Jasmine Flower between herself and Nigel.

'I don't know what on earth you're talking about,' she declared.

'Seems quite clear to me,' said Nigel. 'Clear as the jolly old daylight! I'm talking about our engagement. "A marriage is arranged" and all that tosh! Come on, Mariella, old girl – when is the wedding to be? As soon as I'd decided last night that you were the girl who was going to be the future Lady M., I said to myself: "Can't be too soon! No good hanging about. May as well get the jolly old knot tied sooner as later." So how about naming the day? Next month too soon?'

By this time the shock had worn off a little, and Mariella realised that Nigel had once again decided to take the law into his own hands, and this time it was her life that was going to be forfeit.

'I told you last night, Nigel, that I wasn't going to marry you,' she said firmly.

'All girls say "no" at first,' declared Nigel, unabashed.

'No, they don't, Nigel – not nowadays. *I* don't, anyway. I meant what I said, really I did. I can't marry you, Nigel,

32

you see, because I'm in love with somebody else.'

If Mariella thought that this statement would put Nigel off, she was mistaken. Opposition always made him keener. Moreover, Mariella had, so he argued, put herself in the wrong.

'Been flirting with me, have you?' he exclaimed. 'Making me think you cared for me when all the time . . .'

'I *did* care for you!' broke in poor Mariella.

'And for other people, too, seemingly,' declared Nigel. 'I think what you deserve, my girl, is a good beating!'

Once upon a time, Mariella would have been thrilled at these words. Nigel being masterful! But now she wasn't. Cavemen were all very well in books, but not in real life. Not to marry, anyway.

'How dare you call me a flirt!' she exclaimed indignantly.

'Well, my dear' – the same sweet word that Robin had used, but how different it sounded on Nigel's lips – 'what does one call a girl who leads a chap to think she cares for him – shows him by every means that she adores him – makes his mother think she's in love with him (oh, yes, the mater knew all right – has done for ages!) – all his friends – the whole neighbourhood . . .'

Poor Mariella was silent. The dreadful thing was that such a lot of it was true. She *had* done all those things, but that had been when she'd been in love with the boy she thought Nigel was. But how was she to explain this to Nigel?

'I – I'm sorry,' she faltered lamely.

And then suddenly Nigel changed his tactics. All the charm he had inherited from his ancestors he now turned full upon Mariella.

'Mariella, my darling,' he said in his golden voice, that even now thrilled her, 'you *will* marry me, won't you? If you turn me down, it will be the end of me, I promise you. I shall go to the dogs!'

33

If Mariella had been in a calmer frame of mind, she would have seen the humour of this statement. She might even have added: 'Oh, Nigel – but what about the poor horses? Surely you aren't going to leave *them* out?' But all she heard was his golden voice beguiling her – bewitching her – and felt the net closing round her. To put it another way, the poor fish was being drawn inexorably towards the bank.

'No!' she said, with a last despairing struggle.

The line slackened a little. Nigel knew just how to play a fish.

'*Please*, Mariella. If you knew how much I loved you—'

Nearer the fish was drawn to the bank! Nearer! – And then, just in the nick of time, the situation was saved – by Nigel's mother!

'Oh, Mariella dear,' broke in Lady Monkhouse, reappearing round the end of the stable-yard. 'I've brought you a copy of the evening paper. The notice of the engagement – *your* engagement – is in. I thought you'd like to see it.'

'My engagement! *Who* put it in?' demanded the outraged Mariella.

'I did, naturally,' answered Lady Monkhouse. 'The very moment Nigel told me he'd decided to marry you, Mariella, I drafted it out. I'm really very pleased he's chosen *you*, my dear. You'll suit me very well as a daughter-in-law. Some girls would want to run things all their own way, but I know you'll be only too pleased to let me advise you. For of course (just between ourselves), you *haven't* been brought up to be *quite* what Nigel's wife, the future Lady Monkhouse, should be, have you, my dear? But never mind – between us we'll win through. And there's one thing,' she added, 'we shan't have to worry about those wretched kennel-maids, since you're so good with horses and dogs. Between us we'll be able to cope.'

In a flash Mariella saw her life at Bychester Tower as Nigel's wife. Lady Monkhouse intended to stay there too, and boss the whole show, just as she had done ever since the day when Nigel's father had married her and brought her there. She, Mariella, would be 'young Mr Nigel's wife', and people would whisper behind her back: 'Of course, young Mrs Nigel has nothing to do with the running of Bychester, or with village affairs. You'd better ask old Lady Monkhouse. She's boss at Bychester!' Yes, so it would be! As she stood there beside her horse, Mariella saw into the future. She'd be unpaid kennel-maid and groom. She'd be unpaid secretary too, writing Lady Monkhouse's notes for her, going to the Women's Institute when Lady Monkhouse had something more important to do, and standing back when she hadn't. She'd be general factotum, putting up with Lady Monkhouse's frequent fits of bad temper, and taking the blame whenever anything went wrong. And as for Nigel's golden voice, his good looks – what were they, when there was no real kindness behind them? It was kindness that got you through the world, thought Mariella. Someone who would make allowances; someone who would be a friend, as well as a lover.

'I can't marry you, Nigel,' she said flatly. 'I told you so last night, and I meant it. I shan't change my mind.'

Lady Monkhouse stood there, feet apart, the newspaper in her hand, and goggled (really that was the only word to describe her blue eyes nearly starting out of her head in sheer astonishment). Mariella *not* going to marry her son? Impossible! She couldn't have heard aright! Why, half the girls in the county were out to catch him. The poor girl didn't realise what she was saying.

'But everything is settled,' she said. 'The notice of the engagement is in the paper—'

'Then it must be taken out again,' said Mariella. 'I mean, it must be contradicted. You put it in, Aunt Phyllis, so it's your place to do so.'

'The mater would never do that,' interposed Nigel. 'It

would make her look ridiculous. You wouldn't want to make the mater look ridiculous, Mariella . . .' He appealed to Mariella's chivalry. 'A proud woman like the mater.'

'I'm sorry,' said the girl firmly, 'but she put it in so she must take it out.' She mounted her horse and sat there for a moment or two looking down at them both . . . Nigel, the young squire of Bychester, the son and heir, standing there in the courtyard of his ancestral home, tall, fair, curly-haired, handsome as a Greek god. His mother in her thick tweed skirt, thick knitted green stockings encasing thick sturdy legs. The incredulous expression in her protuberant blue eyes would have made Mariella laugh at any other time. She'd been so certain that *any* girl would jump at her eligible, good-looking son. She'd certainly counted her chickens before they were hatched this time! Mariella almost felt sorry for Lady Monkhouse, now that she wasn't going to be her mother-in-law. It must be a dreadful shock to her!

'I'm sorry, Nigel, if I've misled you,' she said at length. Then she pressed her heels into Jasmine Flower's flanks and rode away, leaving them looking after her.

'And that,' she thought with a sigh of relief, 'is that! There's only the wretched notice in the paper to contradict, and if Lady Monkhouse doesn't do it, I shall just have to do it myself.'

It was when she was nearly home that she once more remembered her aunt's note that she was to have given to Lady Monkhouse. All day long she had carried it round in her pocket! She went back to the post-office, bought a stamp, stuck it on, and dropped the letter in the letter-box with a sigh of relief.

Chapter 5

After Events

Mariella didn't sleep soundly that night. Her dreams were haunted by a Nigel who wouldn't go away, but chased her down endless corridors, and was always just on the point of catching her. Then she would wake up to find herself crying. Sometimes there was a tall, soft-voiced Scotsman in the background of her dreams, but between him and her there was always a wide and dangerous water-jump. (It never occurred to her in her dream that a water-jump was a strange thing to find in the middle of a corridor!) Behind her was Nigel on his horse . . . Her only chance was the jump . . . she felt herself lifted by Jasmine Flower . . . she was soaring, soaring . . . crash! She was down! . . . She woke to find the wind rattling the dead twigs of ivy against the window-panes.

In the morning she was weary and heavy-eyed, which was not at all like Mariella, but then she'd had two disturbed nights, whereas usually she slept like a top. As she dressed, the happenings of yesterday came back to her. There had been a dreadful scene with Aunt Carol, who couldn't and wouldn't believe that Mariella had really refused Nigel, her favourite nephew. Why, she'd exclaimed, Mariella had always been head over ears in love with the boy, ever since they were children. Many a time she'd been sorry for the child because Nigel (as is often the case with thoughtless young men) had failed to come up to scratch in some small particular. But now that he had offered Mariella his hand in marriage . . .

'I just don't understand you, Mariella,' she had said. 'Why, you've always been in love with Nigel. In fact, sometimes I've even thought you were in danger of running after him.'

'Oh, Aunt Carol!' poor Mariella had expostulated.

'Well, perhaps not actually running after him,' had amended her aunt, 'but you certainly did wear your heart on your sleeve. However, I say no more since it evidently hasn't put Nigel off, and he's still going to marry you . . .'

'But he's *not* going to marry me!' Mariella had broken in. 'At least, I'm not going to marry *him*.'

And so it had gone on. Mariella had said some rather rude things to Aunt Carol about trying to run other people's lives (and apologised afterwards), and Aunt Carol had said some bitter things about the ingratitude of Mariella (and hadn't apologised afterwards). She'd also pointed out to the girl the disappointment she would cause so many people to feel – herself, her mother, her uncle—

'Leave me out, please, Carol,' Uncle Harold had said quickly. 'I think Mariella is old enough, and sensible enough, to manage her own affairs. And as for Irma – I hardly think she would see in Nigel the virtues you see, my dear.'

Mariella had been so surprised and grateful that she'd run from the room quickly, so that they might not see the tears running down her cheeks. She had cried nearly all night, and that again for Mariella was something very unusual. No wonder she was white and washed-out this morning!

She went down to breakfast after everyone else had finished, and, to her horror, found her place at table piled up with letters. Of course! The engagement notice! She'd forgotten all about her many friends who must, by this time, have read it. She began to open them, and after the first half-dozen began to look bewildered. And no wonder! They might all have been written by the same person!

38

Evidently all the girls of Northumberland were of one mind. Here, for instance, was Ann Musgrave's (typical of the rest).

'Dear Mariella,' wrote Ann. 'What a surprise when I opened this evening's paper, although of course I'd been half expecting it! I always knew how keen you were on Nigel!' (I shall be called a flirt for evermore, sighed poor Mariella.) 'Oh, Mariella, you lucky, lucky girl! Imagine being the future Lady Monkhouse and living at that romantic Bychester Tower, and being the Lady of the Manor! And fancy walking down the aisle with Nigel! . . .'

Yes, it was quite clear that all the girls for miles around had been imagining this thrilling event, with themselves acting the chief part, thought Mariella with a twist of her lips. The unkindest cut of all was a polite, stilted little note from Robin Campbell wishing her every happiness, and assuring her that he was 'hers sincerely' . . .

'It's too awful!' cried poor Mariella aloud. 'Aunt Phyllis, how could you do such a wicked, wicked thing! . . . Oh, Robin, my dear, what must you think of me?' Leaving her breakfast untasted for the second morning running, she was about to run upstairs and change into riding clothes (riding seemed to be her only escape from the perplexities of life nowadays!) when she realised that a second pile of letters – typewritten, this time – was also addressed to her . . . Messrs Wanless of Newcastle (Court dressmakers) wished to make her wedding gown. And what about the bridesmaids? And of course, that most important lady, the bride's mother? . . . There were firms who wanted to photograph her; firms who wanted to decorate the church, and her home (as well as herself), with flowers. There was even an enterprising tourist agency who would take the happy pair to Sunny Sorrento, or Lovely Lugano, for their honeymoon. And there was a strictly realistic insurance agency who offered to insure the wedding against the 'unpredictable English weather'!

'What am I to do?' cried Mariella in despair, when, as if in answer to her thoughts, the telephone rang. 'Yes, who is it? Mariella Foster speaking.'

A female voice at the other end said: 'Good morning, Miss Foster. I'm from the *Northumbrian News*.' (Goodness! Of course Aunt Phyllis had almost certainly had the announcement put in the morning paper as well!) The voice went on to ask for details of the bride-to-be's-family, and please would Miss Foster tell her something about the bridegroom. 'Something personal, I mean,' she added. 'Of course, we know all about the Monkhouse family. Such a well-known one in the county, and since you are going to marry into it, we thought—'

'Excuse me,' interrupted Mariella in desperation, 'but I am *not* going to marry Mr Monkhouse.'

There was silence, then an audible gasp at the other end.

'Not?'

'Yes. I mean, no. It was all a mistake,' went on Mariella hastily. 'The announcement, I mean—'

'You mean it was rather premature?'

'No, I mean it was wrong. Incorrect, I should say. I'm not going to marry Mr Monkhouse now, or ever. Please, please, put that in your paper, Miss whoever you are. Put it on the very front page! Put it in large red letters, if you like!' cried the overwrought Mariella. 'Only put it somewhere where *everyone* will see it!' She slammed the instrument down upon its cradle, and turned once more to dash upstairs, nearly knocking down Bessie, her aunt's cook, who was standing there.

'Oh, I'm so sorry, Bessie . . .'

'I just came to congratulate you, Miss Mariella,' said Bessie. 'We've just seen the paper. And that goes for the rest of the staff too. We hope you'll be very happy with Mr Nigel . . .'

'Oh!' cried Mariella wildly. 'Will it never stop! Bessie it's all a mistake. I'm *not* going to marry Mr Nigel – or – or anybody. Please tell them that – in the kitchen, I mean.'

'Yes, Miss Mariella,' said Bessie sedately, and retreated. Not her place to exclaim (as she felt like doing): 'Good for you, miss! I thought you had more sense than to marry the likes o' him!' Once on the kitchen side of the baize door, however, her sedateness vanished.

'Well! Would you believe it!' she exclaimed to her companions. ' "I'm not going to marry *nobody!*" Those were her very words. And the whole thing in the papers as large as life. "A marriage 'as been arranged" . . . Could ha' knocked us doon wi' a feather! Must ha' changed her mind overnight.'

'And I don't blame her neither,' put in Wilfred, the gardener-handyman. 'Right sorry I was to hear that Miss Mariella was to marry that young man. Known him since he was a bairn, and a more bossy youngster you'd go a long way to meet. Used to lead poor little Miss Jane a dreadful life! And you know what they say – a leopard canna change his spots. Miss Mariella's too nice for the likes o' him.'

It was decided unanimously in the kitchen that Mariella had escaped something. (Trust the servants to know the true characters of the people they serve!)

'But I still canna understand why she put it i' the paper,' said Bessie.

'I'll tell ye,' said Jennie, who was kitchen-maid and housemaid combined. 'It'll ha' bin that old cow of a Lady Monkhouse! Remember what Harriet Dickson said aboot her when she was kennel-maid up at Bychester? I'll lay a hundred to one she put the notice in hersel'.'

'But why should she go doin' that?' persisted Bessie.

'Anything her darling son wants he must have,' said

Jennie (hitting on the truth, more or less), 'so she tries to rush poor Miss Mariella off her feet. Well, speaking for ma'sel, I'm all for Miss Mariella and her other young man.' (Yes, they all took it for granted that there *was* another young man at the bottom of the affair, and here again they were not far wrong, though Mariella was not quite the heartless flirt they imagined.)

Meanwhile Mariella had escaped from the house and was running down to the stables. She passed the garages on her way, and outside the nearest one stood her uncle tinkering with the car.

'Oh, hullo, Mariella! Just the person I was hoping to see,' he exclaimed. 'You off for a ride? Good! I should stay out for as long as you can if I were you. Let things settle down! . . . By the way, I'm just off to Bridgend. I'll call at the *Northumbrian News* office, and have that notice contradicted, shall I?'

'I've already done it,' said Mariella, laughing hysterically when she remembered the horror-stricken voice of the reporter. 'But perhaps it would be as well if you did it too, thank you, Uncle. And thank you for sticking up for me last night.'

'I felt that there had been a bit of "sweeping the girl off her feet" in a certain quarter!' laughed Harold Foster. 'By the way, Mariella, don't think too badly of your aunt. She didn't mean all the things she said last night. She was a bit het up, you know. She's always been fond of Nigel, and you're very dear to her, too, Mariella, though I know it didn't sound like it last night. You see, she thought at first that her dream of you and Nigel making a match of it had come true, and then to find that it hadn't after all – well, the disappointment was too much for her.'

'Oh, Uncle,' cried Mariella, 'I do seem to have caused a lot of trouble, but really I don't see how it was my fault, unless it was my thinking I was in love with Nigel for so long. But what's worrying me now is what on earth I'm going to do until term starts and I go back to Edinburgh. It will be too awful – all these people being curious – wanting to know . . .'

'Yes, I've been thinking about that,' answered her uncle. 'It seems to me that your best plan just now, Mariella, is to beat an orderly retreat. In other words, go home for a while.'

'Home?' echoed Mariella. To her, as we have said, Monks Hollow was home, though of course, strictly speaking, her real home was in London.

'Yes, to Fortnum Mansions. You'd be out of reach of all the busybodies there,' went on Harold Foster. 'It's a pity you couldn't have gone back with your mother yesterday. I think she said she would be in town for some time.'

Mariella nodded.

'Yes, till after the New Year, anyway. Then she's off to New Zealand. You're right as usual, Uncle Harold. I'll go home until term starts.'

'I'll book a sleeper for you for tonight then, shall I?' he offered. 'I can do it from Bridgend station. It will save a lot of argument if we present a *fait accompli*.'

'Oh, thank you, Uncle!' said Mariella gratefully. 'Not only for arranging about the sleeper, but for *everything*.'

Chapter 6

New Year in London

So it was that Mariella found herself back where she started – at 140a Fortnum Mansions. She slept in the same little bedroom where she had slept as a child. It had French windows leading out on to a balcony, and when she leaned over the railing she could see London spread out at her feet – a cold, foggy, grey London in contrast to the glittering blue and white Northumberland that she had left. But at least it was peaceful! This may sound a strange thing to say about the heart of London, but it was true. Crowds of people there might be, but they were all intent upon their own business, and none of them cared a jot, or were the least bit interested, in one unhappy girl and her love affair. Mariella might just as well be on a desert island! She could go where she liked, and do what she liked, and no one stared at her and whispered behind her back: 'That's Mariella Foster, the girl who treated that nice boy, Nigel Monkhouse, so badly . . . yes, the engagement was in the paper and everything. Shocking, wasn't it? . . .'

Nothing material seemed to have altered the least little bit, thought Mariella, looking down from her balcony. The only changes, as far as she could see, were that the big block of flats opposite had been painted pale blue with scarlet window boxes, and her own little bedroom had been newly decorated by Harridges – pale blue and scarlet, also. (They must have had the flats in mind!) There were new curtains, and the eiderdowns on the twin beds had been covered to match. The pale carpet had been cleaned and had that brushed-the-wrong-way look produced by cleaners! There were photographs everywhere, and here she saw many changes. Some of them (mostly snapshots) were of herself. Mariella on horseback; Mariella at the Rothbury Races; at the Tynedale point to point; Mariella at the meet (actually taken on the day little Meg Mainwaring met with her accident, and Nigel had ridden with Imogen, the child's mother, thought Mariella with a twist of her lips). There were many large photographs of Jane – studio portraits of the famous Sadler's Wells ballerina in her various rôles, and one tiny snapshot of Jane, the engaged girl, leaning against Guy, her fiancé, and looking outrageously happy. There were photographs of Caroline Scott in Spanish costume (strange to think that Caroline had lived here too!) with her Spanish dancing partner, signed across the corner 'Rosita & Angelo' in Caroline's big, generous handwriting. There was a large photograph of Irma Foster, Mariella's famous mother, over the mantelshelf. Mariella had never seen it before, so it must have been taken quite recently. 'She never looks any older,' thought Mariella, 'and yet what an exciting life she's led. It's strange to think of all the exciting things that have happened in this flat. All the famous people who have lived here. If the walls could speak, what tales they could tell!'

And now it was New Year's Eve (Hogmanay in Scotland), and everybody was bent upon enjoying themselves. Mariella's mother was the guest of honour at a big party to be held on the stage of the Sadler's Wells Theatre after the performance. Her father, Oscar Deveraux, the famous ballet critic, was to be there too, and an invitation had been pressed upon Mariella, but she didn't want to go. She had never liked the stage or anything to do with it.

'But won't you be lonely, darling?' asked Irma anxiously. Preoccupied though she was, she could see that her daughter was far from happy. Mariella hadn't told her

45

exactly what had brought her to London so suddenly, but it was plain to anybody that she was suffering from some sort of mental strain. 'I don't like leaving you all by yourself on New Year's Eve.'

'I shan't be alone,' Mariella assured her mother. 'I shall turn on the television, and watch the New Year in with thousands of other people – at second-hand!'

'Well, if that will amuse you—' said Irma, with an inward sigh of relief. Mariella was a bit of a problem at times. She didn't seem to 'fit in'. Never had, in fact. 'You can order a meal to be sent up here,' she added. 'Or of course you can go down to the restaurant, but it might be rather dull all by yourself – most people will be in parties.'

'I'll be all right,' Mariella said again. 'I'll have a glass of milk and a sandwich, and go to bed at midnight, after I've seen the New Year in.'

But in the end, she didn't turn on the television, or go to bed either. Feeling restless, she went out into the frosty night (the fog had cleared away as darkness fell), hopped on a bus, and found herself in Piccadilly Circus, along with several thousand other people, all intent upon seeing the Old Year out and the New Year in, with the biggest possible noise. They were certainly having fun – especially the Scots – thought Mariella enviously. A group of people near her were dancing round in a ring, and singing Scottish songs. As they struck up with Auld Lang Syne, someone saw her standing disconsolately by herself and drew her into the ring.

'Should auld acquaintance be forgot,' yelled her new-found friend. 'Are ye all by yoursel', lassie?'

Mariella nodded. It was no use trying to make herself heard.

'That's no a guid thing for ye at Hogmanay.' His round, red face beamed goodwill towards all mankind. From his waistcoat button floated a balloon in the shape of a haggis.

'Sing up, lassie!' He encouraged her by bawling:

'There's nae luck aboot the hoose,
There's nae luck at a'
There's little pleasure in the hoose
When oor guid mon's awa'.

'Come on, noo! Let's hear ye sing, lassie!'

'Oh, where, tell me, where is your Highland laddie gone . . .'

Suddenly Mariella felt desperately homesick. Her thoughts flew back to Northumberland – to the little surgery at Hordon Castle, where Robin Campbell might at this very moment be treating some poor dumb creature – perhaps the same little kitten that had been the unwitting cause of all this upset.

'A bonnet wi' a lofty plume, and on his breast a plaid,' sang the Scot.

'And it's oh! in my heart I lo'e my Highland lad.'

Yes, she did love him truly, her big, softly-spoken, gentle Highland Robin!

'Ye're no going hame already?' exclaimed the Scot, as she withdrew from the circle. 'Why, ye've no seen the New Year in yet.'

Mariella smiled at him wanly – there was so much noise she couldn't make herself heard. Besides, there was a lump in her throat. She threaded her way through the surging crowd towards the subway. Hundreds of balloons rained down upon her from above. One bounced on her shoulder and she caught it. It was shaped like a chimney-pot, and 'Lang may your lum reek' was scrawled in black letters upon its side.

Everyone was gay and full of fun, thought Mariella. Only she, in all this great crowd, was sad and homesick. But here she was wrong. On the opposite side of the circus stood a

47

small, pale girl who looked much younger than her fifteen years. Ella was all alone too. Patience, her friend, had gone to the party at Sadler's Wells (she'd been accepted for the Theatre Ballet, and was to start in a few week's time.) Patience had been very excited about the party. Irma Foster, the world-famous dancer, was to be there with her husband, Oscar Deveraux, the ballet critic. Patience had seen these people at Jane's wedding, of course, but that wasn't the same as seeing them in their own surroundings. Veronica Weston was to be there, too, with her famous conductor-husband, Sebastian Scott. In fact, everyone who was anyone in the world of Sadler's Wells ballet would be there. It was an awful shame Ella couldn't come, but tickets were limited strictly to members of the company, and Patience had had an awful job to wangle one for herself.

So this was how Ella came to be standing all by herself in Piccadilly Circus, while the riotous, sentimental Scots sang in Hogmanay with their sad, nostalgic songs. Now, it was:

'I'll tak' the high road, and ye'll tak' the low road,
And I'll be in Scotland afore ye.
For me and my true love will never meet again
On the bonny, bonny banks o' Loch Lomond.'

'Only with me, it's Loch Awe,' said Mariella aloud, as she dived into the almost deserted tube. 'And to think that last New Year I was actually dancing in Robin's own hotel at Inveross, on the shores of Loch Awe. I hadn't even met Robin then. All I was thinking about was whether Nigel would take me home or not!'

On the opposite side of the Circus, Ella stood for a while, watching the crowd. Then, with a little sigh, she went slowly back to Carsbroke Place, which was only five minutes' walk away. Her supper tray was laid out in the vast, empty, dining room, and she ate her sandwiches by herself before going up to bed. Mariella got back to the flat

48

at a quarter to twelve. She made herself a hot drink, and turned on the television. Might as well see the New Year in, since it was only another fifteen minutes. On the screen, people were having a wonderful time at a Hogmanay dance in Glasgow. As the midnight hour approached, the fun grew fast and furious. Now they had all joined in a ring, and balloons and streamers had been released from the ceiling . . . something was ringing . . . At first Mariella thought it was in the television programme, then, with a shock, she realised that it was the telephone in the flat, and she got up to answer it. Whoever could be ringing up at this time of night? It was, most likely, a wrong number.

'Regent 269473,' she said into the receiver. 'Mariella Foster speaking.'

A pause. Then the operator's voice: 'A personal call for you, Miss Foster, from Northumberland. A Mr Campbell wishes to speak to you.'

'Robin!' cried Mariella. Her spirits rose in an instant, up and up, until they were among the stars. 'Oh, Robin, you don't know how lovely it is to speak to you! I've been so lonely – so miserable.'

'I am wishing you the very best of everything for Hogmanay!'' said the quiet, kind voice at the other end of the wire. 'It is great good luck that I have managed to catch you. I was sure you would be at a party.'

'Oh, no – I haven't been feeling like parties,' sighed Mariella. As she stood there with the receiver to her ear, she felt it was too wonderful to be true. Here was Robin talking to her – and not on the cheap rate, or on a 'reversed charge' call as Nigel would have done. Alas! How the short three minutes flew! In no time at all the pips sounded.

'Oh, good-bye, Robin,' began Mariella, but the soft voice at the other end went on talking . . . Six minutes! . . . Nine minutes! . . .

'Well, I will say *au revoir*,' said Robin at length. 'I am

49

wishing you all the very best for the New Year. I shall be coming up to Edinburgh soon, when I shall hope to see you. Goodbye, *mo chridhe!*'

'What was that you said?' asked Mariella.

'I am saying *mo chridhe*, which is the Gaelic for – well, I shall not be telling you the English for it over the telephone, but some other time. In Scotland, I think!' There was a laugh in his voice.

She guessed what *mo chridhe* meant. It meant 'my darling'. It meant that Robin loved her! Oh, she was a lucky, lucky girl! Robin loved her – she knew it now! She put down the receiver, her hands trembling, and collapsed upon the hall seat because her legs felt weak.

Chapter 7

By the Shores of Loch Awe

If it hadn't been for that telephone call, Mariella would have spent a miserable and lonely few weeks in London. To many people, a holiday in London spells happiness, but to Mariella it was the dullest place on earth – a place of hustle and noise, crowded streets crammed with hooting cars, and buses, and jabbering people. A place of grey skies, fogs, roof tops, and chimney-stacks, and shop-windows full of stupid fashionable clothes. Far too many evening dresses, and cocktail suits, and far too few really sensible clothes, like mackintoshes, riding-breeches, and tweed coats. At night, neon lights put out the moon and paled the twinkling stars. An awful place, thought Mariella! All of which goes to prove that it's indeed a good thing we don't all think alike. Dutifully she went shopping on the rare afternoons when her mother was free; went to plays and concerts with her father; went to the ballet to see Veronica dance the leading rôle in *Giselle*. She quite enjoyed watching ballet, as long as she didn't have to do it herself. It was fun seeing Sebastian conduct again. He was always at his best when Veronica was dancing. Mariella and her father went backstage after the performance, and talked to Veronica and her young husband.

Veronica had changed, thought Mariella, since the birth of her baby. She had lost the touching quality of extreme youth, but something even better had taken its place. She was now a mature *artiste*, able to portray to the full the feelings of tenderness and love. Sebastian, on the other hand, was the same old Sebastian. He hadn't changed a bit, thought Mariella, as she watched him. Same dark blue sparkling eyes, same crooked mouth, same biting, sarcastic tongue!

'Hullo, Mariella!' he exclaimed. 'Putting up with dirty old London for a bit? Can't imagine how you exist in the place. Too dashed noisy! Too many beastly people!'

Mariella couldn't help laughing – it was exactly what she had been thinking.

'Don't take any notice of him,' put in Veronica. 'He's always like that after a performance. It's a form of reaction. Do you know, Mariella, before the show tonight, I rang them up at home, just to see if everything was all right, and guess who answered the phone? Yes, my little Vicki! Oh, well, perhaps not exactly *answered* it, but she did make the sweetest noises!'

Yes, Veronica was just like any other mother, thought Mariella, even if she *did* happen to be a world famous ballerina!

The days dragged slowly by (oh, how quickly they would have fled, up in Northumberland, sighed Mariella!), but at last she was in the north-bound train, speeding up to Edinburgh. From the window of the dining-car she watched the well-known landmarks fly past – York Minster, Durham Cathedral and Castle upon their hill, with the leafy woods below, and the River Wear winding round them in a great loop. Then came Newcastle with its old cathedral-church, crowned by the famous lantern-tower, and the murky Tyne spanned by its many bridges. Up through Northumberland sped the Flying Scotsman (living up to its name!).

At last she was back in Endinburgh, and at work again. The following weeks were as happy for Mariella as the last had been miserable. For one thing, it was spring in Edinburgh, and flowers bloomed and birds began to build their nests in sight and sound of busy Princes Street. Oh, lovely, lovely northern city, thought Mariella, with its backcloth of blue mountains, its flowers, its historic streets, and, last but not least, its kind people with their lovely, soft, Scottish voices! Of course there were hooting buses and cars here too – she had to admit it – but it was so easy to get away from them into the solitude of the King's Park, where one could be really alone.

And then Robin came to see her as he had promised, and together they did all the things Mariella loved. They walked down the Royal Mile, and peeped into all the old 'wyndes', and explored the quaint corners of which Edinburgh is full. They went to the zoo, and fed the sea-lions, and saw the comical penguins marching in solemn procession, like little old men. They danced Scottish dances together in the gardens in Princes Street by the light of glittering strings of fairy-lamps. They climbed up to Arthur's Seat, for old time's sake; they went down to Portobello, and explored the funny old-fashioned promenade, and swam in the magnificent swimming pool. Oh, the fun they had! Robin, being a canny Scot (using the word in the Scottish sense of cautious), had not yet told Mariella that he loved her in so many words, but she knew that he did, and she made the most of this lovely time before their love was openly declared. Once they were engaged, a little of the magic would vanish – it could not be otherwise. Outside people would know of it, and mundane problems would creep in – the date of the wedding; who were to be the bridesmaids, how many there should be, and the colour of their dresses. All very exciting, of course, but not quite so delicate or romantic as this 'just before the engagement time'.

At the end of the summer term, Mariella went with Robin to his home at Inveross on the shores of Loch Awe. Together they drove round the loch, and, leaving the car parked on the wide grass verge, they walked side by side up the disused railway track towards Coire Chreachainn. It had been raining, and the waterfalls of the Allt Chreachainn, and the Allt Mhoille were roaring and foaming over their rocky beds. At the head of the corrie a great peak stood out black against the sky – Stob Diamh, one of the seven tops of the main Cruachan range.

'How different it all is from that time eighteen months ago when poor Jane got lost up here,' said Mariella as they sat on the hillside admiring the view. 'It's so warm, and peaceful, and friendly today. Then, it was a dreadful wilderness of misty peaks, howling wind, and snow. Poor Jane – no wonder she was terrified!'

'Yes, these mountains can change very quickly,' said Robin. 'Even in the summer time they can be awe-inspiring indeed.'

There was silence between them for a long time. And then suddenly they became aware of a noise above them, and a commotion in the heather. Instinctively they both stood up, and, as they did so, they beheld a very strange and frightening sight – two dog foxes locked in mortal combat, rolling over and over, as they snarled and bit at each other. On a nearby crag stood the vixen, nonchalantly watching her two suitors fighting for her. When she saw Mariella and Robin, she disappeared like a shadow into the bracken. Not so the two male foxes. They continued their fight with complete indifference, right up to Mariella and Robin's feet. Indeed, if they hadn't moved back quickly, they would have bumped into them!

'Robin!' cried Mariella in terror, for indeed the snarling animals looked ferocious in the extreme.

'It is all right, *mo chridhe*,' said Robin. 'They will not hurt you. They are too intent upon their own love affair!'

And then suddenly Mariella realised that she was in Robin's arms, and that he had kissed her, and was asking her to marry him.

'For a long time now – in fact, ever since I saw you standing in Charlton's courtyard that day with your little sad face – I have loved you, Mariella,' said Robin. 'All this time you have been to me *mo chridhe* (which means in the Gaelic "my darling"), even when I could only call you that to myself, thinking that I had lost you. But now, what I must know is whether I mean anything to you?'

'But of *course* you do, dear Robin,' answered Mariella. 'I think I must have loved you, too, for a very long time – in fact I think from that same day, only I didn't know it. I was so used to thinking I was in love with Nigel!'

'Then all is well between us, Mariella,' said Robin. 'And now, when shall we be married?'

'Oh, let's be like Jane and Guy, and have a Christmas wedding,' said Mariella happily. 'I know it's unusual, and that June is the proper month, but you can't imagine how much I envied Jane and her Swiss honeymoon, and the skiing. Can you ski, Robin?'

'Oh, yes – I have often skied in the Cairngorms,' said Robin, as they walked back down the corrie.

'Then you can teach me to ski,' said Mariella. 'And in return I shall teach you how to ride.'

'You may find that a little difficult, my darling,' laughed Robin. 'Highlanders and horses do not seem to mix well!'

It wasn't until afterwards that Mariella realised that animals had played a strange part in her life. First of all, a small, injured kitten had been the innocent means of her seeing Nigel in his true colours, and now two quarrelling foxes had caused her to seek shelter in Robin's arms! Two dog foxes fighting for the same vixen! There was something symbolic about it. She couldn't help telling Robin.

'I do hope I'm not exactly a vixen,' she added, laughing.

'Shall I tell you what you are?' said Robin. 'Then listen, *mo chridhe*' . . . And he told her.

Part Two

Chapter 1

Sunday

And now it is full summer, and once more we meet Timothy
Roebottom tinkering with his car. Once more he is
whistling cheerfully – even more cheerfully than he had on
that winter's day six months ago, because last night, in the
lane by the side of the church, he'd met her again – his
Cinderella! All these months – ever since the Charlton-
Foster wedding – he had sought vainly for her, and then,
suddenly, when he was thinking of something else altogether, he had bumped into her. She'd turned out to be the
kid he'd bought the grey and white ballet dress for, years
ago. 'Life's rummy!' thought Timothy. 'Who would have
thought that that plain, miserable little kid in the church
would one day turn into a ballerina! I wouldn't have
believed it, if you'd told me. Oh, well – glad her name's
Rosetti, and not Sordy. Not that a name matters, of course,
but those Sordys – never could stand them! Fat, giggling
kids, and a Mam with a face like a newly baked brick . . .
going to meet her this afternoon . . . Ella, I mean,' he
added, cleaning the plugs with a bit of cotton rag (couldn't
take a girl like Ella out in a car with mucky plugs!). He'd
persuade her to come along to the church concert on Friday
and dance for them. People would flock to see her – Ella
Sordy of Pit Street – now Ella Rosetti of Sadler's Wells.
She'd make oodles of money for church funds (Timothy,

the vicar's son, always had one eye on church funds!).
Moreover, he, Timothy, would see her dance again. The
thought of it made him clean the carburettor as well. (Must
have the old bus running sweetly for Ella!)

'Timothy!' came Mrs Roebottom's voice from the door.
'It's nearly time for church, dear. Old Mr Whitgift has just
sent Johnnnie with a message to say he's got a bad leg and
can't play the organ, so I'm afraid—'

'OK, Mother, I'll play it,' said Timothy, pushing the car
back into the garage in case it rained. That was the best of a
pocket-size car – you could wheel it about by hand!

Still whistling, he slammed the garage door, and went
into the kitchen to wash his hands.

'Right-ho, Mother,' he said again, seeing Mrs Roebottom
anxiously waiting at the front door. 'Shan't be two secs.!'
He strode into the old-fashioned sitting-room and opened a
music-cabinet with a carved front, and green plush shelves
labelled respectively: ballads . . . manuscript . . . religious
music. From the last shelf he hastily ran through a pile of
tattered music (though 'tattered' is really the wrong word,
since it had been carefully mended, time and time again,
with gummed music-paper).

'The Maiden's Prayer', said Timothy aloud, 'Vespers at
Eventide' (no, that would be better for Evensong), 'Gavotte'
by Mendelssohn.' (Yes, that would do. Brighten 'em up a
bit!) He rummaged in his trousers' pockets. Collection?
Yes, he'd got some. Couldn't afford to put in much – not
this month, anyway. Perhaps next—

'Coming, Mother!' The front door slammed. The house
was suddenly empty. In the room Timothy had just left, the
little Chinese mandarin on the bamboo table nodded his
head and grimaced. Plaster rattled down inside the wall-
paper. The church bell from across the way began to ring
. . . Ting! Tang! Tong! . . . Ting! Tang! Tong! in a rather
cracked tone. A couple of lads, who had nothing better to

58

do, walked past the vicarage and rattled their sticks (cut from the hedgerow) against the railings, and cat-called. It was Sunday at Blackheath.

While Timothy and his mother sit in the little church in the colliery village of Blackheath, let us take the opportunity to fly over to a big country house in the wilds of Northumberland. In a guest-room at Bracken Hall lay Ella Sordy (her real name, as we know, was Rosetti, but she hadn't yet got used to calling herself this). She was quite exhausted by mental strain, and by her adventures of the last few days. Her dreams were coloured by her flight from London on the northbound bus, her arrival, unheralded and unwanted, at Pit Street, the derisive giggles of Lily and D'reen when they had seen her . . . 'Mam! Mam! Here's our Ella! She's come back from Lunnon, and she talks that funny!' . . . Me Mam's assertion that she 'wouldn't see her beat', that she could 'gan up to the Cottage 'Omes', or else 'lie on the floor along o' Lily and D'reen'; the dramatic arrival of Sebastian, who had carried her off in his low, shining black car, just like a fairy tale prince. But no, there was another fairy tale prince, the curly-haired lad who had found, and treasured, her ballet shoe . . . Ella's lips moved in her sleep. She was dreaming of Timothy, now, and the grey and white ballet dress – her very first ballet dress. Her lips parted in a smile, and her eyelids fluttered open.

'Oh!' said Ella, sitting up in bed and looking round. 'Where am I?' Then she remembered everything. She hadn't been sent home from the Wells in disgrace. It was a mistake – her own stupid mistake! She'd thought they hadn't wanted her, whereas it seemed they wanted her very much indeed. They'd said . . . Ella lay there and went over in her mind all that the wonderful Mr Scott had read out to her from the Wells School report: 'This pupil is one of the most promising we have had for a very long time . . . in our opinion no money spent over her dancing education will be wasted . . .' She couldn't believe that they had said this about her. It was too wonderful! Yet Mr Scott had said it so it must be true. Ella, you see, had implicit faith in the dynamic Sebastian Scott!

She hadn't a wrist-watch, so she had no idea what time it was. She got up, found a pale green porcelain wash-basin tucked away in an alcove, washed in it with joy (it made your hands look lovely when they lay in it – like water-lilies!), then dressed, and went over to the window. Her friend, Patience Eliot would have done this first, and leaned out in her lacy nightgown to catch the morning sun, but not Ella. Not for nothing had she spent her early years in Pit Street where night attire was 'not decent'!

Below her lay the Bracken Hall gardens. Ella had never seen anything like them. Dewburn (Patience's home) was lovely, and so was Monks Hollow where Jane lived. But Bracken Hall . . . it was quite impossible to describe the infinite charm of this old house and its surroundings, the way the bracken clothed the hills which curved round it like an amphitheatre; the beautiful effect of the hills themselves, with that little black peak sticking up like the beak of a bird (that peak was Corbie's Nob, though Ella didn't know its name), the belt of dusky fir woods sheltering the house from the cold east winds. The gardens lay in a dewy silence, and below her window was a little rose-garden, and the scent of the roses drifted up to her on the breeze. She leant far out over the window-sill, and away in the blue distance, caught the glint of water. A lake! Oh, lovely, lovely Bracken Hall, thought Ella. She opened her bedroom door, and ventured out into the corridor.

Last night she had been too tired to notice her surroundings, but now her large, dark, wondering eyes took in everything. It wasn't a bit like Lady Bailey's big London house, all soft carpets and cushions, and cream paint.

Bracken Hall was almost austere. Ella didn't call it that, because she had never met the word, but she felt, nevertheless, that the charm of the square hall, panelled to the ceiling and polished until it shone like a lake and reflected the great vases of flowers that stood at the foot of the stairs and in the fireplace, was a charm not to be bought by money. This charm was the result of hundreds of years of polishing, of mellowing, of being loved and taken care of by the generations of Scotts who had lived in this beautiful old country house. Each one of them had added something of his or her own personality to house and garden. One of the Scott ancestors had made the walled-in kitchen-garden, and had grafted the mistletoe on to the gnarled apple tree. Another had laid out the little Italian garden with its fountain. Sebastian's mother, just before she died, had planted the rose-garden that bloomed in loveliness beneath Ella's window. The drawing-room, which Sebastian had made into a music-room, had once been the pride of a long since dead Selina Scott, who had spent long hours playing the spinet, and embroidering the tapestry that covered the wall in the smoking-room, and portrayed one of the family ancestors struggling with a mythical dragon. It was meant to be the dragon of greed, but Sebastian declared that it had much too kind a face – he could have done it better himself!

But to go back to the hall. Ella advanced cautiously down the shallow staircase, and stood at the bottom, looking about her. At the far side, a *barre* had been placed, and above it was a print of the famous Lavery picture of Anna Pavlova in her Dying Swan dress. Over the mantelshelf was another picture – this time of a small, pale little girl darning a ballet-shoe. It was obviously an original. Over by one of the long, mullioned windows stood a grand piano with gleaming lid upraised. At the bottom of the stairs stood a large jug of blue-grey pottery filled with pale mauve, white and pink flowers. They were like butterflies, thought Ella, gently touching one with her finger.

'Yes, they're lovely, aren't they?' said a voice over her head. 'quite my favourite flower.'

Ella jumped.

'Oh, Mr Scott! I thought there was nobody here.'

'Well, there wasn't – until a split second ago, when I arrived. I slid down the banister – didn't you notice?' Ella didn't know what to say to this. He was so obviously 'having her on', but she didn't like to say so. Fortunately he didn't seem to expect an answer, but went on talking. 'Have you had any breakfast, or do you feed on honeydew – like Kubla Khan?' Then, as Ella had obviously never heard of Kubla Khan, he added: 'Or perhaps you feast on beauty – these mallows here? Veronica's hunter loves them, and would snaffle the lot whenever he passes down the drive, if I wasn't there to keep an eye on him.'

'No, I haven't had any breakfast yet, Mr Scott,' said Ella shyly. 'I don't know what time it is.'

Sebastian consulted his wrist-watch.

'Close on eleven. Now, don't say it!' (Ella had opened her mouth to exclaim at the lateness of the hour.) 'Don't say: "Oh, Mr Scott, is it really so late!" What does time matter on a morning like this? What does anything matter, except the sun, and the roses, and the swim that I intend to have in the lake before lunch?'

'Ooh! The lake that I saw out of my window? Can I come too?' asked Ella eagerly.

'Why yes, my child. Why not? Can you swim?' said Sebastian.

'Oh, no,' said Ella, her face falling. Swimming hadn't been thought a necessary accomplishment in Pit Street, and she hadn't had time to learn in London. In Pit Street you 'cleaned yourself' at the sink in the kitchen with a bit of carbolic soap, and dried on the communal roller-towel behind the door, and on Saturday night you had a bath in the scullery in the same water as Lily and D'reen with a bit more hot added if you were lucky. This was all the contact you had with water in Pit Street. To swim in a real lake in your own grounds, with the real trees all around, and a tiny beach of silver sand all to yourself (Ella had caught a glimpse of it from her window) – no wonder she said 'ooh!'

'Do you have a costume?' said Sebastian. 'Swim-suit?'

'No, Mr Scott,' said Ella sadly.

'No matter,' said Sebastian. 'You needn't look so down-cast. (You know you have a very revealing face, like Veronica!) My wife has several. She'll lend you one of them – you're about the same size. And by the way, let's drop the "Mr Scott" shall we? I'm known everywhere as Sebastian. Everyone calls me that, so why not you as well, Ella? Otherwise I shall be forced to call you "Miss Rosetti", shan't I?'

Ella blushed. Here was Sebastian Scott (world-famous, and her hero, to boot) casually suggesting that she should call him by his Christian name! He'd be suggesting that she called his wife 'Veronica' next!

'And another thing,' went on the young man, as though he were a mind-reader, which indeed he often was, 'while we're on the question of names, you mustn't call my wife "Mrs" – she loathes it! She's Veronica Weston – Veronica to you.'

'You really mean it?' said poor Ella in bewilderment.

'Dear lady, do I look as if I would deceive you?' said Sebastian.

Ella stared at him. Deep blue, sparkling eyes; crooked mouth; arrogant tilt of black head. She thought that nothing was more likely!

'I – I'm not sure,' she stammered.

Sebastian burst out laughing.

'Poor little Ella! All right, all right! You ask Veronica, my child, *then* you'll find out that I speak the truth. And now, away to your breakfast! I shall see you by and by – down beside the lake.' He strode over to the piano, opened it, sat down, and a flood of liquid notes filled the panelled hall. Ella stood rooted to the spot. It was like a moorland stream falling into a mossy pool – like one church bell heard from the top of a high hill – like frozen dewdrops falling into a crystal goblet – like . . .

'*Prélude* – Chopin,' said Sebastian, looking round. 'Scoot, Ella! Begone!'

Obediently Ella scooted.

Chapter 2

Veronica's Baby

What a lovely day she had! First, there was breakfast in a sunny room, gay with chintz curtains and chair-covers. Drawn up to the table was a high-chair with a baby in it – a little girl with black hair, and blue eyes, and a strong will of her own, or so it seemed. It was a few moments before Ella tumbled to it that this, of course, was Vicki, Veronica and Sebastian's baby.

'Hullo, Vicki!' she said. Ella loved babies.

The baby smiled an enchanting smile, showing pearly white milk teeth. Then, with a swift dramatic gesture, she swept everything off the tray in front of her on to the floor with a scream of joy. Luckily there was nothing breakable! Ella couldn't help laughing. Just so could she imagine Vicki's father, Sebastian Scott, dealing with a pile of music, when he was working in his study!

'Mink!' said the baby, drumming on the tray with her tiny fists. 'Mink for Vicki!'

'She means milk,' said the elderly nurse, bustling in. 'As a matter of fact she ought to have finished her breakfast long ago, but she likes to be different from other people, don't you, my darling?'

'Mink!' said the baby with outstretched arms. 'Sottis!'

'She means sausage,' explained the nurse. 'Mr Scott will insist on giving her some of his own, and of course she's far too young, but she seems to thrive on it!'

Ella stared at the baby, and thought how strange life was. Here, in this one tiny baby, was Sebastian with his dramatic gestures, his imperious will, his round black head. And here was also Veronica with her pale oval face, her tiny expressive hands, and her lovely smile. One minute the tiny Vicki was the image of her dynamic father, the next the model of her lovely mother. It was indeed a wonderful thing, thought Ella, solemnly eating her breakfast.

During the meal, Veronica herself came in. She had already done her practising, and was going to devote the rest of the day to her beloved small daughter, for tomorrow morning early, she must return to London.

'I shall be back again next weekend, sweetheart,' she promised, stroking the soft black hair on the nape of Vicki's neck. 'I come back every weekend by air,' she went on to explain to Ella. 'It seems to be the best idea. I can't bear to take the darling away from this lovely place to a London flat, but what I shall do when the company goes on tour abroad I can't imagine. It will break my heart to leave her behind.'

It was then that Ella got a glimpse of one of the problems that beset a ballerina – the awful pull between family and profession, even when, as in Veronica's case, her husband was in the profession himself.

'I expect she's happy in this beautiful house,' said Ella.

'Yes, but a baby needs her mother,' said Veronica with a little sigh. Then, seeing that the nurse had left the room, she added: 'Before very long she will come to look upon Trixie as her mother.'

'Trixie is her nurse?' asked Ella.

'Oh, yes. Trixie has been with our family – I should say the Scott family – for a very long time,' answered Veronica. 'She was my cousins' nurse – Caroline and Fiona Scott – so of course my husband saw a lot of her when he was a child. When Vicki came along, naturally we wanted to have Trixie as her nanny. It makes all the difference when you have someone you can trust. Still—' She sighed again, then shook back her dark hair. 'Oh, well – it can't be helped. I could never give up my dancing.'

After her breakfast had had time to settle, Ella went down to the lake, accompanied by Trixie and the baby, who was fast asleep now. They were joined halfway down the drive by several dogs, and still later by Sebastian, who had a couple of towels wound round his neck. The lake proved to be as exciting as it had looked from Ella's bedroom window. More so, in fact, since there was a tiny island in the middle of it, and a couple of swans swimming about regally.

'They nest here every year,' said Sebastian. 'There ought to be some young ones somewhere about . . . Oh, there they are! Yes' (as he saw Ella's amazement), 'they aren't very pretty, are they? Cygnets are always like that, you know. They change in due course and become as beautiful as their parents. Ever read Hans Andersen's fairy-story, *The Ugly Duckling*?'

Ella shook her head.

'Well, it's in the bookcase in Veronica's boudoir. She keeps on hoping a choreographer will make a ballet of it for her some day – Toni Rossini, maybe. I know he's toyed with the idea. It's a lovely story, and come to think of it, it's a bit like you. Ugly little brat, if I remember rightly (off the stage, anyway). Quite good-looking now.'

Ella stared at him wonderingly. She supposed he was meaning her, but really his mind flew about so fast, she found it hard to keep up with him. He had now turned to the boathouse, and was drawing her attention to an array of ancient bathing-costumes that hung over the sides of a little rowing-boat.

'Would you believe it!' (He held up a garment of green and yellow.) 'This is Spotted Peril! Oh, I assure you – a genuine Maggy Rouff! Regard the "cut"; the "line". Quite,

quite ravishing, is it not?' He held the object up against his chest and appealed to Ella.

'I think you are making fun of me, Mr Scott – I mean, Sebastian,' said Ella with her shy smile.

'Oh, never, dear lady,' said Sebastian, shocked. 'I, who am the most serious of mortals, make fun? Never! . . . Well, let us doff our sombre, everyday garments, and clothe ourselves in the raiment of water nymphs and – I'm not sure what the masculine of nymphs is . . . Ah! Here comes my wife.'

They all bathed, and Ella had her very first swimming lesson. If she didn't actually take her toe off the sandy bottom, at least she learnt not to fear the water. It was beautifully warm, for the summer had been a hot one. Veronica swam over to the little island, and Sebastian towed Ella across. The dogs, barking with excitement, swam alongside. Then they all sat in the sun and ate wild strawberries, until a silvery chime reached them from across the water, and Veronica said: 'Lunch in half an hour.'

'OK,' said Sebastian reluctantly. 'It's usually I who hear that stable-clock, and drive you home to your milk! Would you believe it,' he added to Ella, 'Trixie still tries to "feed Veronica up", as she calls it, with glasses of milk!'

In the afternoon Timothy arrived, and took Ella for a ride in his car – a gleaming monster indeed, since it had been polished to a mirror-like brightness with a whole tin of his mother's floor polish! They went up on to the moors, along rutted country roads that often deteriorated into mere cart tracks.

'I do hope you don't mind being bumped a bit?' Timothy asked anxiously as they lurched over a particular bad stretch. 'Old boneshaker isn't as young as she was.' (You would have thought from his voice that the car was an aged but beloved relative!) 'Still, the view's fine, don't you think?'

Ella said the view was beautiful. She thought the car was beautiful, too, though it *was* so old the mileometer had been round twice and was now nearing 90,000 yet once more, and its springs seemed non-existent! She wouldn't have changed it for a Rolls Royce. Hadn't Timothy given her a ride in it the very first time they had met? That was enough for Ella! The old boneshaker was her fairy chariot. And as for the view – it was quite magnificent. They parked the car on a stretch of green turf and sat looking down at it. Miles and miles of rolling hills of soft turf, and heather just coming into bloom, with here and there fat crimson cushions of ling and a blazing bush of gorse. The wide grass verges of the road were embroidered with yellow trefoil, and underneath the many stone bridges gurgled the clearest of moorland streams. It was an unfenced road, and small black-faced sheep came and stood in the middle of it and baa-ed disapprovingly at them. In the distance lay the Border hills, fold upon misty fold. Countless miles of wild, lonely country, with not a single house or dwelling of any sort in sight.

'Unless you count a sheep-stell, or a shooting-butt,' said Timothy.

'Shooting-butt? What is that?' asked the girl.

Timothy explained all about the grouse shooting that begins on what is known as 'the glorious twelfth' – the men with the guns – the dogs – the beaters.

'You mean, like Hans Andersen's story about the ugly duckling?' said Ella, who had already found and read the story. 'All the poor birds will be flying about, as happy as happy, and then suddenly, bang! One of them is dead.'

'That's the idea,' said Timothy. 'It's supposed to be great sport,' he added.

'Do *you* think it's great sport?' asked Ella.

Had Timothy but known it, his fate depended upon his

reply. He considered the matter for a moment.

'Can't say I do,' he confessed. 'I think I prefer the bird-watching idea. More interesting, if you see what I mean. But of course, I'm no sportsman. Can't shoot for toffee.'

'Oh, I'm *so* glad! cried Ella with such intensity that he turned in the driving seat to stare at her. 'I'm *so* glad!'

'I see – you don't like killing things?' he said gently.

'Oh, *no*!' said Ella passionately. 'What for did God give them lives, if it was just to be killed?' (When she was excited Ella's English sometimes slipped back to Pit Street).

'Yes, it's certainly a thought,' admitted Timothy. 'But what about the animals who kill each other?'

'They dunna know no better,' declared Ella. 'Besides, they do it so's to live – not just for *fun*. No animal would kill another one just for fun.'

'What about a cat and a mouse?' teased Timothy.

But Ella wouldn't allow it.

'The cat intends all the time to eat the mouse,' she told him.

'And when she plays with it?'

'I expect she's just copying human beings,' declared Ella. 'Anyway, she wouldn't do it if she wasn't hungry, and she dunna know no better.'

'I expect you're right,' laughed Timothy. 'Well, if you've had enough of the view, we'd better be getting on, don't you think? It's feeling to me like tea time!'

They had tea at Wooler at a little café called the Patchpole, because Ella couldn't resist its funny name. It was what is known as a 'plain tea' in these parts, and it consisted of plates of bread and butter (white and brown), several kinds of jam, granny loaf, girdle scones, and fruit cake. They finished off the lot – at least, Timothy did. The waitress wished them good-day, and gave the curly headed young man a special smile (more for himself than for his tip)

70

as she watched him squeeze back into the driving-seat of his pint-size car.

They ran down to the coast at Bamburgh, and stood on the castle ramparts, and watched the waves creaming in over the golden sand. Away on the horizon was a misty blue island.

'That's Lindisfarne,' explained Timothy, 'where the monks lived, and jolly old St Cuthbert. It's only an island at high tide, and now they've built a causeway of sorts, you can get across without getting too wet. Some day I'll take you over in the old bus. That's the best of a car like mine – a wetting doesn't do her as much harm as it would one of your modern, low-slung posh cars, all chromium plate and what not!'

As they drove back, they passed a great square bay of sand covered now by a few inches of sea water in which hundreds of birds were wading for fish.

'This is Budle Bay,' said Timothy. 'It must be close on high tide. It was here, you know, that the Childe Wynd met the loathsome dragon – the "Laidly worm" of Spindleston Haugh.'

'Tell me about it,' ordered Ella.

'Well,' began Timothy, 'the story begins in the usual way of fairy-tales. Once upon a time there was a king who lived in Bamburgh Castle. He was a widower with one beautiful daughter called Margaret. He married a second time (like they all do in fairy stories) and of course the new stepmother ran true to form, and was deadly jealous of her lovely stepdaughter. So, being a witch (they all are in fairy-tales!), she turned the poor girl into a serpent – a laidly worm. "Laidly" means loathsome, by the way. This serpent ravaged the countryside, eating cattle by the dozen, and scoffing a few children by way of dessert! Added to this, she burnt all the good green grass with her fiery breath. In fact, by all accounts the girl turned into a most efficient flame-thrower . . .

71

'Well, when her brother, who was called Childe Wynd (seems an awkward sort of name for the poor chap, but there you are!) heard what was happening, he hurried back from what was known as "them furrin parts", and, in spite of the charms and spells of his wicked stepmother, he beached his ship (which had masts of the rowan tree, gauranteed witch-proof) in yonder sandy bay. The first thing he saw was poor Margaret, tying herself in knots on the beach. Of course it never entered his stupid head that the serpent was his sister, and he was just about to slay the monster when, to his amazement, it began to recite:

' "Oh, quit thy sword, and bend thy bow,
    And give me kisses three:
For though I am a poisonous worm
    No hurt I'll do to thee."

'Childe Wynd, being a simple soul, never suspected treachery as some folk would have done, and he gave her the kisses. In fact, he went the whole hog and put his two arms round her neck, whereupon the worm crawled away into the bushes, and came forth his own beautiful sister Margaret.'

'And what happened to the wicked queen?' asked Ella.

'Oh, the Childe Wynd turned her into a poisonous toad,' said Timothy. 'You see, he was something of a magician himself.'

They left the coast, and drove back to Wooler, and over the moors home again. The sun was setting, a ball of crimson in a duck-egg blue sky, when they drove in through the gates of Bracken Hall.

'Thank you so much, Timothy,' said Ella when they reached the front door and he helped her out. 'It's been a lovely, lovely day.'

'Glad you liked it,' answered Timothy, turning suddenly shy. 'Well, I think I ought to be getting back, and you *will* come over and dance at our concert?' (He had already asked her on the way home).

'I shall love to,' she said. 'Only of course I shall have to ask Mrs Scott – I mean Veronica. We're not supposed to dance in public, while we're at the Wells School. But I know she'll say I can. What shall I dance?'

Timothy considered the matter.

'What about the Cinderella dance – the one of the famous grey and whte dress?' (They had laughed together over the incident.)

'Oh, yes!' Ella's face lit up at the thought of the dress. 'I'd love to wear it again. I only hope it still fits me! I left it at home – at Pit Street, you know. Mam – my mother – said she'd keep it safe for me.'

'OK. How about calling for it before the show?' said Timothy. 'I mentioned the concert to Sebastian, and he said if you promised to dance he would bring you over in the car. I'd come myself and fetch you, only I've got to carry forms, and chairs, and put up curtains, and the Lord knows what before the thing begins. No one else to do it.'

'Oh, I can easily call for my dress,' said Ella. 'I'll not forget – I mean, I won't forget. Goodbye, Timothy. Are you quite sure you won't come in?' she added a little wistfully. She was loath to see her hero depart.

'No thanks,' said the young man. (Mustn't plant himself upon the Scotts for supper, however much he wanted to!) 'Got to get back before lighting-up time. Lamps not too good – except for the fog-lamp, which is super, but one can't drive on a fog-lamp, can one? Well, so long, Ella!'

Ella watched anxiously, as, with a tremendous clatter, and clouds of smoke, he reversed the car, and rattled away down the drive. He waved cheerily to her as he turned the corner, and then he was gone. The world suddenly seemed very empty and a little sad, though of course she would see him again on Friday.

73

Chapter 3

The Concert

'My goodness!' said Ruth Fisher. 'How positively terrifying!' Ruth had done most of the work in connection with the Blackheath parish concert (being producer, choirmaster, and compère, all rolled into one), and she was now busily engaged upon 'making-up' the cast for the play which was to be the main item of the first half.

'What's terrifying?' her friend, Jean Rutherford, demanded, pausing in her task of making up the faces of ten tiny children.

'My dear, you know we are to have Ella Rosetti (you remember little Ella Sordy?) to dance for us? So far, so good – she always *was* a dear, sweet child. But imagine me conducting my ladies' choir, composed of Mrs Duffy, Mrs Minto, and a dozen other canny bodies (as they say round here) in front of the one and only Sebastian Scott! I grow pale at the mere thought! Why, the only one among the lot who can really sing in tune is Cynthia Roebottom, and *her* voice, though sweet, is completely drowned by the roaring of the rest. Gosh! How I wish it was over!' Which was odd, when you come to think about it, because most of the rest of Blackheath (the friends and relations of the children concerned, not to mention the children themselves) were looking forward to this concert, and would certainly look back upon it as the highlight of the year. Far from wishing it over, they rather wished it would go on for ever! But then of course, they hadn't the awful responsibility that weighed upon the shoulders of poor Ruth Fisher. They were not even aware that the famous Sebastian Scott was about to descend upon them. To be quite frank, they'd never even heard of him! So, in this case, ignorance was certainly bliss.

At that precise moment Sebastian, himself, was standing at the door of 113 Pit Street, engaged in a heated argument with Me Mam, who, dressed in her Sunday best (a coat of bright red, trimmed with what looked like sections of door mat), was just about to set out for the concert, for wasn't Our Lily saying her 'piece', and Our D'reen acting in the play? With all her faults, Mam Sordy was loyal to her family. She had no idea, of course, that Ella was going to dance. In fact, nobody knew, except the Roebottoms, Ruth Fisher, and a few intimates. And now here was Ella herself, standing in the doorway, looking that posh, accompanied by that strange young man who had nearly scared the daylights out of her last week, waiting in the road, and tapping impatiently with his silvermounted cane. Whatever would the neighbours think? They'd imagine she'd got 'mixed up in summat'.

'I was just off out mesel,' she said to Ella, 'but if it's all that important, I daresay I can wait five minutes. I telt our Lily to sit on a chair for us at the front. What's the use of havin' a bairn in the show if yer canna get a front seat? Come in wi' ye, then.' She stood back to let Ella enter, but didn't extend an invitation to the young man. 'A dress you was talking aboot?'

Now, Me Mam knew perfectly well which dress Ella meant, and she also knew that it had gone to the jumble sale. But, 'Say nowt, and yer canna go wrong' was Mam Sordy's motto, or, in more civilised language, 'Least said, soonest mended'.

'Yes, Mother – my ballet dress,' said Ella, running up to her little room, and rummaging in the cupboard. 'A grey and white dress. You remember – the one I danced Cinderella in? You said you'd keep it for me.'

'I canna say as I remembers nowt aboot it,' shouted Me Mam from the bottom of the stairs. 'But if you say you left it 'ere, 'ere it'll be.'

'But it isn't! It isn't!' cried Ella in anguish. She had all the temperament of the true *artiste*. Here was real tragedy! You might have thought she'd be glad to get out of dancing at a concert in a pit village at the back of beyond, but not so. It might have been a Royal Command Performance at Covent Garden! Tears streamed down her face. She wrung her hands.

Sebastian, coming to the door to see what was keeping her, and what all the shouting was about, wasn't nearly as much taken aback as you might have expected. How often had he seen Veronica in just such a state! In fact, how often had he been in just such a state himself!

'What's the matter?' he asked. Most of the inhabitants of Pit Street had, by now, gathered in a little knot behind him. They were a well-dressed crowd, because most of them were going to the parish concert. First of all, though, they must see what was happening. All sorts of rumours flew round – Mam Sordy had gone mad, and was beating up that poor little orphan girl . . . The little orphan girl had gone mad, and was beating up Mam Sordy (less likely, but incidentally nearer the truth! Poor Mam Sordy was certainly getting the worst of it). Other views were that a copper from Scotland Yard (Sebastian) was arresting Mam Sordy for some dire crime. They hadn't yet decided what . . . An officer (Sebastian again) from the Cruelty Place (the NSPCC) was 'telling off' Mam Sordy.

Suddenly Sebastian realised the presence of a crowd of women breathing down his neck. He turned round, and the crowd drew back several paces. Whoever this young man was, he certainly commanded respect. They could almost see the handcuffs sticking out of his coat pocket!

'My good ladies,' said Sebastian, 'I don't know what you imagine is going on here' – he waved dramatically at the Sordy dwelling – 'but I assure you that if you think a murder is being committed, then you are wrong, quite wrong. Something has been lost, that is all. No, no – not stolen jewellery. (I can see that some of you are jumping to conclusions!) Merely a ballet dress.'

'Oh, *that*! Why, she sent it to the jumble sale,' exclaimed Mrs Golightly, a bosom friend of Mrs Sordy, but with whom she wasn't on speaking terms at the moment. 'I seed her.'

'The jumble sale!' cried poor Ella, who had appeared at the bottom of the stairs. 'Oh, no, I don't believe it!'

'Come, my child,' said Sebastian soothingly. 'It is time for us to go, if we are not to be late. Another dress shall be found for you. In any case, what does it matter? These people' (he waved at the crowd, which was now dispersing in the knowledge that nothing of real interest was going on at Number 113) 'would not appreciate you. You are casting pearls before swine, my dear.'

Yes, Sebastian could talk like this, when it was somebody else who was performing. Had he been doing so himself, he would have been in a worse state than Ella, who, by this time, was drowned in tears.

It was Cynthia Roebottom who, when they arrived at the church hall a few minutes later, saved the situation.

'Ella's grey and white frock?' she said, when she had heard the sad story. 'Why, my dear – I've got it over at the vicarage. Yes' (as they all broke into excited exclamations), 'I bought it at the jumble sale. I don't know what made me do it, I'm sure. I think it was just the sight of it lying there so crumpled and – well, sort of forlorn and forgotten. Besides, I'd drawn it in my pictures, you see, so I felt the least I could do was to treasure it. Listen! I know what we can do. We'll put Ella's "number" in the second half, and I'll go over to the vicarage now and iron it.'

'I'll come too,' said Ella.

After this, all was plain sailing. Never had a concert gone off so well! The church hall was packed to the doors, and people were standing, four deep, at the back. The news of Ella Sordy, once of Pit Street, now of Sadler's Wells, had flown round, as Timothy had known it would, and people who would never have dreamt of patronising a church concert in the ordinary way, now came to stare. One after another, they crowded in. Ella's fame rose as her story passed from mouth to mouth. By the end of the evening, she was *prima ballerina* of Covent Garden . . . 'Aye, Mabel, I'm not kiddin'. She's next to – you know that dancer, Margot somebody or other? Well, Ella Sordy's took on some o' her parts.'

'Well – who'd a thought it! Ella Sordy!'

Gloria Sordy (who had married Our Syd, only son of the Sordy family) had come all the way down from the Dun Cow to bask in the limelight of her sister-in-law's fame. Gloria chose to forget the fact that Ella, being the Sordy's adopted child, was really no relation to her at all.

'Give over, our Alfred!' she said to her firstborn, who was insisting upon crawling over the feet of the people sitting in the same row, and giving their ankles a playful nip with his sharp little milk teeth. 'Be a good boy, and take a look at yer ant-y. Reel famous she is!

Ella's solo was clapped to the echo. Not that they understood the difference that lay between her lovely flowing arm movements, the expressions that passed over her rather sad little face, her beautiful, clear-cut footwork, and Mabel Duffy's elephantine gallops across the· stage. Mabel Duffy went to Miss Martin's' ballet school, so she was well-trained, but no teaching on the part of Mary Martin or anyone else could make the portly Mabel light

78

on her feet. The audience merely knew that they liked Ella best. Only Mrs Sordy gave a loud yawn at the end of Ella's dance.

'Prefer tap, mesel', she said, turning to her neighbour on her left. 'What do you say, Bella?' To her surprise Mrs Dickson's eyes were full of tears.

'Got summat in me eyes,' said Mrs Dickson ashamedly. 'Speck o' dust, likely! It's sad that dance, ain't it? Poor little beggar – Cinderella, I mean. Never knew afore how sad it were.'

And, indeed there was something in Ella's dancing that made each member of the audience feel she was dancing especially for her, and herein lies the secret of every great *artiste*. All these people – large, well-to-do women, down-trodden women, women who, you might say, were 'hard-boiled' – felt themselves to be Cinderella when Ella danced.

The concert drew to a close. The conjurer had drawn the last few dozen silk handkerchiefs out of his mouth, and the last hard boiled egg out of his ear. The 'funny man' had told his last story and the last part-song – 'Nymphs and Shep-herds' – had been sung by the buxom members of the ladies' choir, and if it *was* a trifle flat, nobody noticed. The last 'number' had been tapped out by Susie Duffy, in a bright pink frock, and a large pink satin bow bobbing on her brassy ringlets.

But now an extra thrill was in store for Blackheath. The great Sebastian Scott, himself, would conduct the choir. The ladies nudged each other in delight. There now! You see, it took a great man to appreciate good singing. They'd always known they were good! . . .

You might have thought that Sebastian, used as he was to Covent Garden Opera House, and the huge Albert Hall, would have been bored at the very idea of conducting a ladies' choir, composed mostly of pitmen's and iron-foundry workers' wives, in an obscure village hall on the borders of Durham and Northumberland. If you thought this, then you didn't know Sebastian. Sebastian was *never* bored. Annoyed he might be, furious he might be – but never bored. Besides, these dear ladies were enthusiastic (the width to which they opened their mouths, and the way they nodded their heads, testified to that), and enthusiasm is never boring.

'Now we will sing: "There'll always be an England"', said Sebastian. He raised his hands – those wonderful, sensitive hands, every finger of which possessed authority – and they sang. The tin roof of the little hall was nearly lifted off. Never had they sung like this! No longer were they flat. No longer were they a trifle coy. They forgot all about themselves, and just sang.

'All together now! commanded Sebastian. 'Everyone join in. Come along! All the lot of you!' With an all-embracing gesture, he drew in the whole audience – beginning with the children sitting on benches or on the floor in front, their grandmothers sitting squarely on chairs in the body of the hall, and ending with the lads and lasses standing at the back.

'There'll always be an England,' sang Gloria Sordy along with the rest, 'in every country lane.' Her thoughts went back to her childhood when she had gone blackberrying on the moors round Blackheath, and she fancied she could smell the scents of autumn as she sang.

And so the concert ended.

'The Queen!' commanded Sebastian. Then, after they had sung the national anthem, he gave them his usual, formal little bow.

'I thank you,' he said, and stepped down from the platform.

And so Ella went back to the vicarage for coffee and sandwiches. There were cakes, too, from that expensive shop in Newcastle, and chocolate biscuits, and fruit jellies.

Cynthia Roebottom had just received another cheque for her drawings, and she had spent some of the money to entertain Ella, whom she considered was the cause of her good fortune. It wasn't a very sophisticated feast, it is true, but then Cynthia herself wasn't sophisticated; nor, come to think of it, was Ella. Neither of them had ever tasted a cocktail!

They had the meal in the old-fashioned drawing-room with the green plush-covered settee, and the jangly piano. The little Chinese mandarin nodded his head approvingly whenever Mr Roebottom laughed, or Sebastian made one of his dramatic gestures. Things were looking up at Blackheath Vicarage!

'Nice people, those Roebottoms,' pronounced Sebastian, as they drove home. 'Knowledgeable, too. Cynthia took quite an intelligent interest in my views about the modern trend in music.' By which it will be seen that Cynthia Roebottom was a diplomat!

Chapter 4

Flora's Birthday Party

The holidays sped away. Sometimes, when Ella thought about them, they seemed to have lasted for years and years, and sometimes it seemed only yesterday that Sebastian had found her, and brought her to Bracken Hall. But now it was the end of August, and she was due to return to the Wells next week. But before that, there was Flora's birthday party. Flora, who was the only daughter of Fiona and Ian Frazer, had arrived at the great age of two years. Since Fiona was Sebastian's cousin, he insisted upon making the party his own responsibility, and holding it at Bracken Hall. Fiona, needless to say, was only too glad to be saved the bother. She wasn't above making use of the occasion, however.

'While we're about it, we might as well ask a few of the mothers and fathers,' she said, when they met to discuss the arrangements. 'There are the Smith-Carnabys, and the Waybridges, and the—'

'Now see here, Cousin Fiona,' said Sebastian, 'this is a *children's* party, and there are going to be *children* at it – and no one else.' Sebastian had never liked Fiona, and didn't mind her knowing it. 'When I feel like saving you the trouble of entertaining your cocktail-drinking friends, I'll let you know.'

Fiona shrugged her shoulders. She knew (none better!) that if she was rude to Sebastian, he was quite capable of throwing up the whole affair, and she'd be left with Flora's party on her hands. She couldn't cancel it at the last moment either, because, in a moment of thoughtlessness, she had broadcast invitations to quite a lot of children. Oh, well – perhaps the Smith-Carnabys, and the Waybridges, would count an invitation to their children the same as one to themselves!

Flora's birthday fell in the middle of the week, but the party was to be on the Saturday, so that Veronica could be there. It was a never-ceasing source of wonder to Veronica and Sebastian (and everybody else, too) that Flora should be such a good-tempered, sunny little soul. She wasn't at all pretty (having taken after her father in looks), but she had the most charming nature imaginable.

'Far more charming, I'm afraid, than our own offspring,' commented Sebastian, giving an affectionate pat to Vicki's black head as she toddled past him.

'Oh, but Vicki's only a baby yet,' put in Veronica. 'You can't really say she's got a nature.'

'Oh, hasn't she? said Sebastian wickedly. 'Behold, then!' He made a gesture towards his daughter, who, dressed in a morsel of pink embroidered silk and net, was firmly collecting up all poor Flora's birthday presents, and carrying them away to a corner of the lounge, where she stood guard over them. As she had only just started to walk, and wasn't yet very steady on her legs, this was quite a business. Vicki was not one to give up, however. When she dropped anything, she went back for it, and gathered it up jealously into her arms. Meanwhile little Flora watched the proceedings anxiously.

'Vicki's!' said Vicki, embracing all the birthday gifts with a gesture that was very like Sebastian's own. '*All* Vicki's.'

Fiona came flying down the room.

'Veronica, it's disgraceful' she exclaimed. 'That child ought to be soundly spanked. Look what's she's done! She's got all poor Flora's presents . . . yes, what is it?' A little boy, aged about three, was plucking at her skirts.

83

'Look! Look!' The small boy's eyes were round. 'She's giving them all away!'

And sure enough, Vicki, with an angelic smile, was handing out Flora's birthday presents like a queen dispensing largess.

'Vicki give!' she said. 'Vicki give presents!'

'There, you see!' exclaimed Veronica triumphantly. 'I told you! She's a dear, generous little girl.'

'I'm afraid, my sweet,' said Sebastian, with his crooked smile, 'I'm much afraid that she is a little exhibitionist.' He went to the rescue of the owner of the presents, and the excitement died down. But not for long. Things were never without excitement where Vicki was.

'Oh, look, Veronica! I do think you ought to do something about Vicki.' It was Fiona again. All the children were having tea at a long table in the dining-room. Vicki, being the youngest of the party, was perched on top of a mound of cushions. In front of her was a plate overflowing with small cakes.

'She just takes a bite out of one, and then asks for another,' went on Fiona. 'And Sebastian keeps on giving them to her. She's got six already! It's very bad training. Surely you want her to grow up with nice manners – like Flora?'

'Not at all,' answered Sebastian, pressing yet another cake upon his delighted daughter. 'Never had nice manners myself. Always deplorable. Another piece of shortbread, my darling?'

'You *are* naughty, Sebastian!' exclaimed Veronica. 'Really, you mustn't do it. Vicki doesn't understand.' She tried to remove some of the cakes, but Vicki resisted with screams of fury.

'Vicki's tates!' (cakes) 'Vicki's tates!'

'She's a selfish little girl!' said Fiona, with a note of triumph in her voice which said: 'and no wonder – with a father like that.'

84

'You had better leave her alone, my dear,' said Sebastian to his wife. 'After all, this is a party – not a lesson in manners.'

A few minutes later, Veronica, returning from the kitchen with yet another plate of sandwiches for her tiny guests, beheld her daughter handing round cakes (each with a neat little bite out of the side) to her guests in lordly fashion.

'Vicki give tates! Vicki's tates *nice* tates!'

'Anyone would think the other cakes *weren't* nice!' laughed Veronica. Really, you couldn't help being amused at Vicki's antics. 'The other children seem to think they're something special too!' It was obvious that, even at the tender age of one year, the small Vicki was going to be a leader of the human race.

After tea, the party went out into the garden where a Punch and Judy Show awaited them. They sat in entranced rows on the lawn watching the puppets' antics, while Sebastian with his ciné camera took a film of their expressions to show his friends.

'You see! The same old magic!' he said, as the children, with shrieks of laughter, watched wicked old Punch beating his scolding wife. 'It may be a shocking story, with no moral at all, but the young love it!'

After the Punch and Judy Show, they all trooped back to the house to see Veronica dance. She gave them the Breadcrumb Fairy's Variation (now called the Fairy of the Golden Vine) from the *Sleeping Beauty*. Even the very young children sat quiet, lost in wonder at the lovely ballerina. And then, of course, Ella had to dance too, though really it was hardly fair to ask her, after so wonderful an exhibition. She gave them her Cinderella dance, because she was able to dance that in her ordinary cotton frock, and a pair of ballet shoes borrowed from Veronica, who took the same size.

Sebastian, watching her, thought of that Christmas, many years ago now, when Veronica had danced in this same hall, and he had first known that he would surely marry her one day, and that they would come back to Bracken Hall to live. He wondered if Veronica remembered, and looked across at her. But she was watching Ella, and didn't see him.

Chapter 5

Ella Returns to London

Ella's return to Carsbroke Place was quite unspectacular. Lady Bailey had made it clear to the staff that no one was to gossip about the disappearance of little Ella Rosetti. Lady Bailey paid her servants too highly, and treated them too well for her commands to be disregarded, so nobody said a word to her about what had happened. Perhaps Perkins, the butler, was a little less unbending towards Ella than before, and Polly, the pert maid, especially friendly.

'Poor little soul!' she said to the cook while they drank their 'elevenses,' 'she must ha' bin homesick to go all that long way, and by bus too. Always makes us sick, do them buses!'

Ella was now working mostly with the Senior School. Strangely enough, the other students, usually so jealous of every newcomer, were quite fond of Ella. She had ceased to be what Gilbert Delahaye called 'a piece of wet tripe', and was now a gentle, hard-working girl, determined to make her dancing as perfect as possible.

'My dear, I can see in our Ella Rosetti a future prima ballerina,' said one of the students, Ada Right, to her friend, Jill Makepeace, as they waited their turn to practise *déboullés* from one corner of the room to another.

'Well, of course she's Veronica Weston's protégé, isn't she?' answered Jill. 'Trust one ballerina to know another!'

Yes, Ella was so good she didn't even have to push to get into the front row of the classes nowadays. It was taken for granted that she should be there. In any case, they liked to watch her – her 'line' was beautiful.

Ella's fifteenth birthday came and went. She received a birthday gift from Veronica and Sebastian – a short coat made of nylon 'fur', because they both knew Ella's views on real fur coats! Mrs Roebottom sent her a pastel drawing of herself (Ella) as Cinderella. She had done it while she sat in the church hall on the night of the concert. Timothy sent her flowers – fairylike freesias ordered from a London florist, to be delivered on the day. What sacrifices Timothy made to buy them for her will never be known. Me Mam, Lily, and D'reen sent her a birthday card with a funny picture on it of a fat woman bathing. At least, Me Mam thought it was 'a proper scream', and so did Mrs Duffy to whom she showed it before dropping it into the letter-box, but Ella didn't even smile when she took it out of the envelope. Later on in the day, she quietly put it in the waste-paper basket (since there were no open fires at Lady Bailey's). It was sweet of them to remember her but— . . .

Christmas approached. Ella was dancing in the Opera Ballet so she wasn't going home. Her friend, Patience Eliot, was now in the Second Company, so she wasn't going home either. There was one good thing about it, thought Ella. She wouldn't be lonely! The bond of friendship between her and Patience had strengthened since Jane's wedding. Ella had now met many of Patience's friends, and they were able to talk about them. Mariella Foster, for instance. Mariella was going to marry that nice, quiet Robin Campbell, and the wedding was to be on the day after Christmas – just like Jane's.

'I had a letter from Mariella this morning,' said Patience, 'but I've been so busy I haven't had time to read it yet.' She pulled it out of her pocket, and read it aloud.

'Monks Hollow,
Nr Bychester,
Northumberland.

Dear Patience—Only ten days to Christmas! I just can't believe that in less than a fortnight I shall be Mrs Robin Campbell! Robin teases me by saying I shall be known as: 'Herself of Inveross'. But perhaps he isn't joking – Highlanders *are* funny! I mean funny-peculiar, not funny-ha-ha.

'I'm very sorry you can't be at my wedding – and Ella, too – but of course I quite understand. No one can tell me anything I don't know about the demands of a ballet career – I've learnt it all from Mother! It's quite safe to say you can't go *anywhere* you want to, at *any* time you want to! However, I know how much you love it, so perhaps you don't feel quite like that about it. Anyway, I expect you'll want to know all about everything. Well, my wedding dress is to be of thick cream brocade with a glittering golden thread in it, and I'm to carry a sheaf of lillies. My dress is to have a train of lace that Mummy wore when she was married – it's been in the family for a very long time. I'm wearing a shoulder length veil of tulle with a crown of orange blossom, and golden slippers. The bridesmaids are all children. The two bigger ones are Gillian Grey, who often rides to hounds with me, and Meg Mainwaring. The poor child was so disappointed at not being able to be a bridesmaid at Jane's wedding (she got measles at the last minute, remember, and Ella took her place) that I just *had* to ask her to be mine. Anyway, she's quite a nice kid when you get to know her. The baby bridesmaids are Flora Frazer and tiny Vicki. I don't know how they'll behave on the day, but they'll certainly *look* sweet. No one will so much as look at me! They're all going to be dressed in long frocks of cream brocade with posies of lilies-of-the-valley. Oh, and there are to be two

89

pages. One of them is a nephew of Robin's, called Hamish McPhee, and the other is little Richard Craymore. You remember Stella and Jonathan? Well, he's their only son. They're to wear kilts and all the etceteras. The church is to be decorated with mimosa.

'Oh, Patience, I'm the happiest girl! You can't imagine how lovely it is being engaged to Robin. I always know he'll be kind and thoughtful, and that he'll be there when he says he will, and not keep me waiting, and finally turn up with a glamorous female in tow!'

(From which cryptic sentence it can be seen that poor Mariella had suffered much at the hands of Nigel Monkhouse! Mariella went on to speak of Nigel.)

'I hardly ever see Nigel now. When I was first engaged to Robin, he used to come here a lot. I think he imagined I had become 'involved' with Robin, and that sooner or later I should regret my engagement, and turn to him. When I didn't, I think he shrugged his shoulders (mentally) and decided I wasn't worth bothering about. I've never seen Aunt Phyllis (to speak to, that is) from that awful day at Bychester to this. I sent her an invitation to my wedding, of course, but she hasn't even replied. I don't think she'll ever forgive me. I wish she would, though, because I hate quarrelling with people.'

As a matter of fact, Lady Monkhouse had had a busy time during the last few months explaining to her friends all about Nigel's wonderful escape from the scheming Mariella.

'My dear' (in a confidential whisper) 'a girl with a mother on the stage – not exactly the right person for the future Lady Monkhouse . . . Exactly! Just what *I* thought. I knew you'd agree. So it was a blessing I stopped it with a firm hand before it had got too far . . . These young people . . . so impetuous! Nigel was quite fond of her in a brotherly way, but of course there was nothing serious . . . The notice

90

in the paper? Quite a mystery as to how *that* got in. Of course one has one's *suspicions* – some people would stop at nothing to secure a good match for their daughters – but I won't say any more, because one can't *prove* anything, and one mustn't jump to conclusions, must one? . . . Mariella's wedding? Oh, dear me, no! I shan't waste my time going to *that*.'

Some of Lady Monkhouse's friends (those with unmarried daughters) believed this story, but most didn't. Mariella was far too popular to be classed as a scheming minx. But to get back to the letter . . .

'We are flying to Switzerland for our honeymoon,' it went on. 'Not the same place where Jane went, but somewhere else that Robin knows, and where the skiing is wonderful. Robin is going to teach me how to ski. Later on, when we come back, I'm going to teach *him* how to ride a horse, but he says I shall never do it, because Highlanders are just *not* horsemen. I shall have a good try, anyway! After Switzerland, we are going to a little village near Naples for a week, and after that, we must come back, because Robin is a busy man, and, as he says, animals don't stop being ill just because the vet gets married. I think I shall be quite a help to Robin in his work, because although I'm not yet qualified, I know quite a lot about it. I did think of finishing my training, but it seemed such an awful long time – another three years, at least, even if I passed every exam straight off, and I probably shouldn't, and such a lot of money. I don't think I was born to be a "career girl", but just an ordinary domesticated wife!

'Later in the year, we shall go to Inveross, because (as Robin puts it), he must introduce his people to Herself! Oh, Patience, aren't I going to have fun, married to a braw Highlander! You see, I'm learning the language already!

'Well, goodbye, *mo chridhe* (this is the Gaelic for my darling, and Robin taught it to me). Love and every good wish,

'from your happy Mariella.

'PS. Love to little Ella, too.'

Patience folded the letter up slowly.

'Well,' she said, 'I think there's no doubt about Mariella's future. It's sure to be a rosy one when two people are as much in love as they are.'

Chapter 6

The Swan

Nine days to Christmas! The London shops were smothered in tinsel decorations, 'hollied' wrapping paper, Christmas trees, and 'frost'. Some of the windows had little dabs of cotton wool stuck all over them, so that there was a perpetual snowstorm! All day long, crowds of shoppers invaded the big department stores, and were carried up and down on moving staircases and lifts. It seemed to Ella, as she looked at their anxious faces, and the way in which they clutched their many parcels, that some of them were more worried than happy! Still, the children made up for it – especially the tiny ones. As they sat in sledges drawn by reindeers in one shop, or were transported to the moon by a spaceship in another more up-to-date (if less seasonable) one, their faces were radiant with joy.

Ella made her own Christmas presents, buying 'remnants' of silk and fine linen, and covering them with exquisite embroidery. Patience had taught her how to do this (having herself learnt at her French finishing school), but Ella had very soon outstripped her master. Her tiny fingers flew in and out of the delicate fabrics, and produced the most beautiful handkerchiefs, tray-cloths, and table-mats for her friends. As for her beloved Patience, nothing was too good for her. Ella made her a pale blue linen dressing-gown with Richlieu embroidery all down the fronts. Even Patience, used as she was to beautiful things, had never had anything so lovely!

Ella did most of her sewing at rehearsals and between

classes – the only free time she had. You see, although she was in the Opera Ballet, she still attended classes in the Senior School, so, with her, it was work, work, work, all the time! On the few nights when she was not dancing herself, she watched other ballet performances – Margot Fonteyn in the classic rôles, Violetta Elvin, and Rowena Jackson, besides Veronica Weston. Sometimes – not as often as she would have wished – she practised in the studio at the top of Lady Bailey's tall London house. Usually she did it all alone, but on rare occasions Patience or one of the other students joined her, and Lady Bailey would come and watch. She was devoted to the art of ballet, and, as she saw Ella's dancing improve, it thrilled her to know that she was helping to give this beautiful dancer to the world. She, like everyone else, was amazed at the change wrought in little Ella Sordy over the last eighteen months. She was not pretty – she never had been; in fact, many people thought her positively plain – but she was now beautiful. Now, if you think this is a contradictory statement, consider for a moment what prettiness really means. It means regular features, curling hair, sparkling eyes, pink cheeks. Ella had none of these things. Her eyes and mouth were a great deal too large for her small, oval face. Her hair was dark and straight, and shone owing to much brushing, but it did nothing to soften her features. Her eyes were dark and sad; her skin was sallow. Yet there was no doubt at all about it, she was beautiful – especially when she danced. Then her eyes would glow with an inward fire, and her face would light up with a spiritual radiance. Most important of all, there was her exquisite body, tiny, full of grace. Lady Bailey never tired of watching Ella, even when she practised the inevitable *pliés*, *battements*, and limbering-up exercises that are part and parcel of a dancer's life – yes, even when she becomes a ballerina.

At the Wells school, all the dancing staff knew that in Ella they had a classical ballerina in the making. The purity of her 'line', the absence of mannerisms, her beautifully held head, her unaffected hands and arms, her clear-cut footwork told them this. Slowly, slowly, she conquered each movement. Nothing satisfied her but perfection, and her wise teachers were content not to hurry her. They realised the prize they had got in Ella Rosetti. She was now ready for the stage. Not for Covent Garden, but for the Theatre Ballet, known as the Second Company, that practice ground for budding dancers. Here she would gain experience, learn stagecraft – in other words, try out her wings. After Christmas, she would be joining the company. It certainly looked as if there were no breakers ahead in Ella's sea! But there is usually a snag somewhere, and, in Ella's case, it was her health. She was a delicate girl. All those years of bread and marge, with a scrape of jam, that had turned Lily and D'reen into strapping young women, had had the opposite effect upon the less robust Ella. Often, after a hard class, she was utterly exhausted, though during the class itself she never showed it. But Gilbert Delahaye noted her pallor, and spoke of it to the rest of the staff. Her classes were cut down, and she was forbidden to attend the Character classes. She was sad about this, for she loved the gay Russian dances, the Hungarian and Rumanian folk-dances, and, above all, the Spanish flamenco gipsy dancing.

'Well, anyhow, you're better off than Caroline Scott,' declared Patience, when Ella told her of the Wells decision. 'According to Mariella, *she* had an awful time when she was here at the Wells, because she was no good at anything *but* Character dancing. Of course you know that Caroline is the great Rosita now?'

'Yes, I'd heard about Rosita,' answered Ella. 'And of course I've often seen her dance. Do you remember the first time, Patience? It was when Mr Delahaye gave me two tickets and told me to try my luck and ask you to go with me. I had an awful job screwing up my courage, I can tell you!' They both laughed at the thought of it.

'Talking of Rosita,' went on Patience, 'I had a ring from her yesterday. She wants both of us to go and spend the evening at 140a Fortnum Mansions, where she lives, on Christmas Night. Irma Foster is having dinner at the Ritz, so we'll be all on our own– about six of us. Angelo, Caroline's partner, will be there too. Caroline asked me to ask you if there was anyone you wanted to take along – the opposite sex, I mean – but I told her I didn't think so.'

Ella shook her head.

'No one, thank you,' she said. Her thoughts had flown to Timothy, but he was too far away. She couldn't ask him to come all those miles, spending money he certainly couldn't afford, just to spend a single evening with her.

It was on the day before Christmas Eve that the strange thing happened. Classes had finished at lunch time, so Ella travelled back by underground, intending to do a little last-minute shopping. It was about three o'clock when she reached Piccadilly Circus. Overhead, the sky was a cold, steely grey, and a flake or two of snow were drifting down. It looked as if it was going to be a white Christmas.

Ella shivered a little, and coughed. She was just recovering from a dose of flu, and the air was raw, especially after the warmth of the tube. She made her way across the Circus towards Oxford Street, intending to go into one of the big shops there. Although it was not yet dusk, the neon lights were flashing, and all the shops were brightly lit. Ella's thoughts flew back to the home of her childhood – Blackheath. In her imagination she could see again the small, brightly lit shop windows, steamed by the heat inside, but gay nevertheless with festoons of coloured paper streamers. They were full of Christmas merchandise. She remembered especially the 'stockings' made of coloured net, with a gaudy paper figure of Santa Claus stuck on the outside. Inside, were all manner of things – tiny coloured sweets, liquorice all sorts, cheap little toys made of tin, paper hats. Father Christmas had always brought three of them for herself, Lily, and D'reen. They were lovely to look at when they were hanging up at the bottom of the bed, but a little bit disappointing when you pulled out what was inside. Most of it was cardboard and packing paper! Still, she couldn't help thinking of them with nostalgia.

Ella was nearly across the Circus by this time, and she was so deep in her thoughts that when the thing happened she stood stock still, nearly getting run over by a lorry, whose driver leaned out of his cab and shouted at her for her carelessness. But Ella didn't even hear him. She couldn't believe her eyes! Down to her very feet, fluttered a large, white bird, and lay there, obviously dying. It was a swan!

Ella forgot all about the traffic, and gathered the bird up in her arms. We know her views about animals, and all living things. Well, here was a swan, hurt. The traffic would just have to stop, while she ministered to it. And stop it did! If you don't believe me, you have only to read the papers, and you will see that it is quite true . . .

Yes, it was all in the papers! The Queen and the Royal Family read about it in *The Times* next morning. Business men glanced at it in the *Manchester Guardian*. All suburbia thrilled at the story over their afternoon teacups and their bridge tables. Timothy Roebottom read about it in the *Northumberland News*, and the Sordy family in the *Blackheath Gazette*.

'Mam! Mam!' cried Lily, shrill with excitement. 'See here, Mam! It's our Ella! Our Ella wi' a great big swan!'

All the Sordys came running – D'reen in her gym slip, Me Dad in his shirt sleeves, Me Mam still in her curlers

97

(though it was three in the afternoon), and, of course, Lily herself. Lily had left school last term, and was now serving behind the 'fats' counter at the Co-op.

They all craned over the paper. Sure enough, they recognised in the girl on the picture page Ella Sordy, who had lived with them for the first thirteen years of her life, though how they did so, it is hard to say, for the resemblance had by now almost disappeared.

'Traffic held up in Piccadilly Circus!' they read. 'Swan with broken neck dies in ballet dancer's arms. It is thought that the bird came from Regent's Park, and that it must have flown into the telegraph wires in the gathering dusk, and so met its fatal injury. Pathos was added to the scene when the male swan flew down also, and refused to leave its dying mate. The beautiful girl is a dancer at Sadler's Wells, so she told the reporters, and some day she hopes to dance Anna Pavlova's famous Dying Swan' . . .

Oh, the perfidious Press! All this because Ella innocently replied to the question as to whether she had ever seen the Dying Swan: 'Oh, yes, I saw Markova dance it. She was very beautiful.'

By this time the RSPCA inspector had arrived to remove the body of the dead swan, only to be savagely attacked by the male bird. The strange thing was that he allowed Ella to fondle him as she crouched there with the dead bird in her lap. The RSPCA inspector explained to the fascinated crowd that had by now collected round them, that contrary to the habits of most birds, who only mate for the season, the swan mates for life. When Ella heard this, slow tears began to roll down her cheeks. They fell upon the breast of the poor dead swan, and upon the soft white feathers of its bereaved mate as she stroked it.

In a short while, along came a posse of mounted police to

see what was causing the hold-up, and great was their surprise to find a slender girl sitting in the middle of Picaddilly Circus nursing, of all things, a dead swan! However, London police are used to dealing with any and every emergency, and, with the help of the RSPCA inspector, they managed to capture the live swan by throwing a net over it, and to place the dead one in the RSPCA van which had by now appeared on the scene.

'Please, please – would you mind telling me where you're taking him,' begged Ella. She felt as if she were abandoning someone who trusted her.

'Regent's Park, miss,' said the inspector cheerfully. 'That's where he'll have come from. Like to come along too, miss? Right ho – hop in.'

'Oh, thank you so much,' said Ella, and got into the van. The grace with which she did it made the man remark afterwards to his fellow inspector, that there was 'something about that girl', though he couldn't have told you what it was.

And this was how it came about that Ella made friends with the swans in Regent's Park. They soon learned to feed out of her hand, and became very tame indeed. They would even allow her to stroke them. She made friends with the park keeper, too, and he would let her go over to the island, where the swans nested, so that she could study them. Many were the happy hours she spent there. In after years, when she danced the leading rôle in *The Ugly Duckling*, with choreography by Rossini, and people asked her where she had learnt her swan-like movements, she would smile gently and remember these hours she had spent in the park studying the swans.

As for Timothy, after he had read the account of Ella and the swan, he went out into the yard, where his dragon sat waiting his pleasure. He took out the sparking plugs, cleaned them, tested the oil and the battery, and gave her a rub here and a brush there. The old bus must be completely roadworthy. Timothy had a long journey to make.

Chapter 7

An Evening of Dancing

Christmas Day in London! You could hardly believe that this was the same city as the hurrying, jostling, noisy, busy city of the night before. Now, all the church bells were ringing, and the only people in the streets were those hurrying to morning service. Snow had fallen during the night – just a light powdering – and the footsteps of the worshippers made a black and white pattern on the pavement. Soon the church doors would be shut, thought Ella, as she followed the crowds of people streaming into St Martin-in-the-Fields, and all those footprints – big and litte – would be a silent witness that this was Christmas Day.

It was a beautiful service. The vicar gave a simple, heartwarming sermon instead of a learned address. While he was speaking, a little grey London sparrow flew into the church, and perched on the altar rails. Some clergymen might have been shocked, and beckoned to a verger to deal with the interloper, but not the vicar of this church.

'God loves all the things that He has made,' said the vicar. 'Not only does He love human beings, but He loves the birds and the bees, the animals in field and jungle, the fish in the sea, the birds in the air, like this little sparrow. God loves all living things. It must be so, or He would not have given them life.'

Ella and Patience walked home after the service. Passing Trafalgar Square, they stopped to feed the pigeons.

'After all, it's Christmas for them too,' said Ella, and her thoughts were on the vicar's sermon. In fact, though she did not realise it, this sermon had a great effect on Ella's life.

It was when they got back to Carsbroke Place that Ella saw a curiously familiar vehicle parked outside Lady Bailey's house. It was a car of an exceedingly ancient make, painted a cheerful red, and with a fog-lamp of great brightness on the front. Getting out of it was a large young man, walking rather stiff-legged, as if he had travelled a very long way. He looked up at the dignified façade of Number forty-two, and it was then that Ella saw his face.

'Timothy!' she exclaimed, hardly able to believe her eyes. 'Why, it's Timothy! However did you get here? Did you come all that way in your car?'

'Hullo, Ella,' said the young man, pulling off a huge and ancient driving-glove, and shaking hands. 'Merry Christmas! Yes, I came in the old bus. Did it like a bird – no trouble at all, except for a couple of punctures, and a leaky pump. Soon got that fixed up. Started off yesterday, and travelled through the night. Easier with the old bus – she's not so hot in traffic, you see.' (You would have thought he was talking about a live horse, thought Ella. Dear Timothy!)

'You *must* be tired,' she said, full of concern for him. 'All that long way, and it's nearly lunch time! Do come in. I know Lady Bailey would want you to stay for lunch – she's such a darling. Oh, of course you know Patience?'

'How do you do, and a Merry Christmas,' said Timothy, enveloping Patience's hand in his own big warm one. 'Yes we've met before – at Charlton's wedding. Thanks awfully, Ella – a spot of lunch sounds just the ticket. Oh, no, not tired at all. Quiet pleasant, really, driving through the night. No traffic to speak of. Dropped off at a church in Oxford at seven this morning and made my communion.'

They went into the house – the two dancers, and the big

young man, who had just travelled three hundred miles through the night, carrying out running repairs on the way by the light of a torch and the moon, to see his best girl. But bless you! What is three hundred miles to a young man of Timothy's age? He'd have travelled twice that distance and thought nothing of it!

And so Ella had a wonderful Christmas Day after all. They rang up Caroline and told her of Timothy's arrival, and Caroline said it was most fortunate, because Angelo's friend had got flu at the last minute, so they were a man short, and Timothy would just save the situation.

Before they set off for the flat in Fortnum Mansions, Timothy had to see all Ella's Christmas cards, and there, right in the middle of the front row, was the one he'd sent her – a picture of the manger, with a frosty sky that glittered, and a covering of sparkling snow on the ground.

'Dad says snow is very rare in those parts – especially at Christmas time,' said Timothy, surveying his card and its position on the mantelpiece with a glow of satisfaction and pride. 'But I think it's very effective myself – the glittering frost – and anyway, one must allow a little licence.'

'Oh, I think it's *lovely*,' said Ella. 'Quite the most beautiful one of all my cards.' (As if she wouldn't have thought the same of any card Timothy sent her, even if it had been the cheapest!)

Then, out of politeness, Timothy had to take an interest in Patience's cards, which were arranged on the top of the grand piano. They were far more expensive and more numerous than Ella's, and some of them were real works of art. But all Timothy saw, as one after another was pointed out to him, was Ella's gentle, pale face, and her great dark eyes looking at him so kindly. Patience had many lovely presents, too. All the expensive things that well-off girls give to each other – tiny exquisite trinkets of silver and enamel, handkerchiefs dark with Swiss embroidery, more

102

handkerchiefs with borders of real lace. Tiny flaçons of Parisian scent from her French friends, hand-printed scarves. David, her brother, had sent her an evening bag of *petitpoint*.

'By the way, what did your father give you?' asked Ella, suddenly realising that she hadn't seen any gift from Colonel Eliot to his daughter. 'I expect it's something lovely.'

A cloud came over Patience's face.

'He sent me a cheque,' she said. 'I expect he thought it was safer. Father wouldn't know what to buy me.' She gave a little sigh, and Ella knew that Patience would rather have had a simple gift that was the result of a little thought, than all the money in the world.

After lunch they walked into Regent's Park and fed Ella's beloved swans, and of course Timothy had to be introduced to Hector, the swan that had featured in all the newspapers.

'Poor Hector is a widower,' said the girl, 'so I always keep a special piece of bread for him.'

They walked round the rose gardens, and Ella thought how strange it was to think that, in a few months' time, all these cold frozen beds would be blazing with colour.

In the evening they went to Fortnum Mansions, where they found Caroline and Angelo awaiting them. Angelo's friend, Toni Rossini, the well-known dancer and choreographer, was there too. Both Ella and Patience knew him, so they were a merry party. They had dinner downstairs in the restaurant – turkey, and plum pudding blazing with brandy, carried in by the chef. The room was decorated with holly and mistletoe, and a great Christmas tree, on which hundreds of little coloured lights winked and blinked, stood in the centre. It took Ella's thoughts back to Pit Street, and the little tree in the window of Number 113.

It was nearly ten o'clock when they went up in the lift to

103

the flat, which was on the fourth floor. While the young men chose records for them to dance to, Ella, Patience, and Caroline went to Irma Foster's bedroom where Caroline said they would find plenty of costumes to wear.

'Aunt Irma never minds me, or my friends, using them,' she added. 'She doesn't need them, now that her career as a dancer is finished.' The words sounded sad, but of course they were true. A dancer's career is indeed a short one. Only twenty years at the very most – from eighteen to thirty-eight.

All along one wall of Irma's lovely bedroom were built-in cupboards crammed with costumes. Underneath, were rows of square boxes containing *tutus*, some old, some new, which Irma had worn for practice, or for her own use. Patience found a black one with a glittering bodice, which had evidently been for the rôle of Odile in *Lac des Cygnes*, and Ella took out a delicious white one with panniers of pink net, which enclosed her slender form like the petals of a rose.

'I shall dance the Rose Fairy variation out of the *Sleeping Beauty* in this,' she said.

Caroline had disappeared into her own bedroom, and now she came forth in Spanish costume – a bouffant skirt with a wide flounce of black lace, and little red shoes with high heels. Her hair was parted in the middle and bound to her head severely, and behind her right ear was a red rose.

'I shall give you the Miller's Wife from *Le Tricorne*,' she said, 'if we can find the music. Angelo could play it, but he is needed as my partner . . . And do you know a rather wonderful thing has happened. They are doing a new production of *Le Tricorne* at the Wells, and Angelo and I have been asked to be Guest Artists in this ballet – I am to dance the Miller's Wife, and Angelo, of course, the Miller. You should see his *farruca* – it's superb! It seems quite wonderful that I should be turned out of the Wells because I wasn't good enough, and then go back as Guest Artist!'

After they were all dressed, they went into the lounge, where they pushed back the sliding doors that divided the room into two parts, and rolled back the rugs. Patience, in her black *tutu*, sparkling with sequins, executed the famous thirty-two *fouettés*. Ella, dewy as a rose in her pale costume, provided a complete contrast as she danced the Rose Fairy variation. After this came Caroline, dark and vivacious as the Miller's Wife, and Angelo dancing his *farruca*, passionate, sultry, quiet, violent – all in the same wonderful Spanish gipsy dance. Angelo was at his best in flamenco.

Sometimes they danced to records, sometimes Toni played for them, and once when Toni, dressed in pale tights and white-sleeved blouse, partnered Ella in a *pas de deux* from the *Sleeping Beauty*, Timothy played for them. He had no idea he could play so well! Perhaps it was the lovely Bechstein piano (certainly the tinkling, green-silk-fronted instrument in the Roebottom's parlour didn't make the best of one's talent!), or perhaps it was because he was playing for Ella. Whichever if was, he surprised both himself and his friends with the tenderness of his playing.

The party broke up at one o'clock in the morning. Before they left, they sent off a communal telegram to be delivered at Monks Hollow in the morning, for tomorrow was Mariella and Robin's wedding day!

Next morning Timothy arrived at Carsbroke Place just after breakfast, saying that he must go home.

'It's just been a flying visit, I'm afraid, but it's been worth it just to see you, Ella. Well, so long! Got to be back at work in the morning, you see.'

'But I thought – I mean, the Cambridge term—' began Ella. Timothy cut her short.

'I've come down from Cambridge,' he said simply. 'Pipped my exams.'

'Come down from Cambridge?' Ella's eyes were wide with horror. 'Oh, Timothy, why? What happened!?

Standing on the steps of Carsbroke Place, Timothy told her. Ella, reading between the lines, saw clearly what had happened, though Timothy would never have admitted it. It amounted to this. Timothy had been president of the debating society, vice-president of the union; he was a cricket 'blue'; he'd stroked his college boat to victory (and had been carried shoulder-high). Yes, every honour had been heaped upon Timothy Roebottom, except that of his degree. The latter hadn't been afforded him. Perhaps too much time had been taken up with social activities; perhaps (Timothy's own explanation) he hadn't been clever enough. Whatever the reason, the sad fact remained – he'd pipped his exams, ploughed, come a cropper! No second chance was his. He might, of course, have got a place in another college, but it wouldn't be a 'grant' place, and it would cost a mint of money. Mr Roebottom had wanted to make this sacrifice for his only son, but Timothy would have none of it.

'No, Dad,' he had said firmly. 'Sorry, but can't be done! Just can't allow it, that's all. Should never have gone up in the first place. Knew all the time I should never stay the pace. Got to have brains – and plenty of them – nowadays. Just haven't, that's all! Would never have thought of Cambridge, but knew how disappointed you'd be if I didn't go up to your old college. Sorry, Dad – should have worked harder, I expect, though, as I say, it just isn't in the old brainbox.' His face looked suddenly old and haggard, and Mr Roebottom put a kind hand on his son's shoulder.

'Never mind, Timothy,' he said. 'It's no use crying over spilt milk! We'll see you through somehow. We'll manage. Your mother—'

'Cut that out! exclaimed the young man. 'I'm not taking any of Mum's hard-earned cash, and that's flat. I may be all kinds of a lazy hound, but I'm not a sweep as well.'

'All right, all right, leave it over the weekend, and we'll have another talk about it,' said his father.

So they left it over the weekend, and on the Monday, Timothy disappeared in his car. He came back whistling. He'd got a job with an engineering firm in Newcastle.

'A whole lot better at engines than history, Dad,' he said cheerfully. 'From now on I pay my way here – understand, Mum?' He put a strong young arm round his mother's waist and fox-trotted her across the room. 'Gosh! I'm as happy as a king! No more swotting! No more end-of-term exams!'

So Timothy worked for a while in the machine 'shops', and got very dirty, and was very happy. He loved engines (always had!), and they loved him. They ran more sweetly for him; less noisily; more economically. In other words, they purred for him! His sensitive hands coaxed them to run faster and more smoothly than they had ever done before. He got more and more interested in them. He began to invent ways of improving them . . .

'Keep an eye on that young chap, Roebottom,' the shop stewards and managers of the departments began to say. 'Got a genius for invention has that lad! Shouldn't be surprised to see him going places!'

They were right! Timothy found himself back at college – King's College, Newcastle, this time in the faculty of engineering – at the firm's expense. He found that studying history from a matter of duty was a vastly different thing from studying engineering because you were wildly interested in it, and wanted to find out everything about it. He came down from King's with first-class honours! A few years later, he was awarded his Ph.D.

Dr Roebottom! Nobody was more surprised than Timothy to hear himself so addressed! Blackheath didn't know what to make of it. They'd written off Timothy Roebottom as a failure, or worse! (Stories had gone round that he'd been sent down from Cambridge in disgrace.) Now, here he was, 'Dr Roebottom'! Blackheath decided that there was something 'phoney' about the whole thing, and that Timothy wasn't a real doctor, but only a makeshift.

But all this is in the distant future, and at the present moment we are still on the steps of Carsbroke Place, and Timothy is trying to convince Ella that he is happier – oh, yes, very much happier – in his new job than he ever was up at Cambridge.

'You see, I *like* messing about with engines,' he told her. 'They seem alive to me – not like a lot of dead and gone history!' Which goes to show that it takes all sorts of people to make a world.

Chapter 8

The Cat

People with sensitive natures suffer a great deal in this world. Their hearts are constantly being torn by the cruelties they see around them. It's so much easier for you if you are insensitive, but how much worse for the world! Ella, too, had a tender nature. She was as brave as a lion in defence of the weak and tormented, though ordinarily she was gentle and timid in the extreme. If she had lived one hundred years ago, she would have pitied the little chimney-sweeps, the bare-footed crossing-sweepers. Her heart would have bled for the children, sent, at eight years old, to work down in the coal mines, never to see the light of day. Indeed, she would certainly have been one of them herself! If she had lived in the reign of Queen Victoria (or even later), she would probably have been sent out to 'service' at the age of twelve. She would have spent her life in a dark cellar kitchen, called (very appropriately) 'below stairs', and there she would have toiled, from five in the morning till ten at night, carrying heavy trays of dishes and buckets of coal, up and down the many flights of stone steps, painstakingly whitened by her own coarse, red, little hands. She would probably have slept down there too, all among the Victorian black beetles. On Sundays she would have been allowed to go to church, where she would have sat at the back in decent humility, dressed in sober black as befitted her 'station in life', and woe betide her if she had the temerity to pin a flower in her bonnet!

Yes, the world is a much better place to live in nowadays,

thanks to those sensitive people, whose efforts overcame the evils they saw around them. But there is still room for improvement. It was the animals that concerned Ella. Not people's pets, but the strays – the mangy cats sitting at street corners with rheumy eyes; the miserable dogs hungrily gobbling refuse out of dustbins, and those chained to kennels in people's back yards; the songbirds in too-small cages. All these things she saw as she walked to and from her ballet classes and rehearsals, and they tore at her heart. If it hadn't been so, she wouldn't have been the *artiste* she was. When you see a brilliant *artiste*, who, for some reason, fails to move you, you will know that she is either one who is slow to develop, and is as yet 'unawakened', or (more likely) that she is insensitive. It was the infinite compassion in Ella's soul that made her dancing beautiful to watch.

One November evening, when she was returning from rehearsal at Hammersmith, she happened to be passing a badly-lit street at the corner of a bomb-site. The tenants had been moved to a new housing estate, and so the buildings were empty, and were awaiting demolition. A little knot of people stood at the corner of the road, obviously discussing one of the houses, since they kept pointing at it, and looking up at the windows. As she passed, Ella heard the words '. . . cat . . . yes, the people left it behind . . . ought to be ashamed of themselves, leaving the poor thing to starve . . .'

Ella stopped, and joined the group.

'What was that you were saying?' she demanded. 'Did you say there was a cat in there? A cat, starving?'

The people turned round and stared at her, taking in her lovely fur coat (they thought it was fur, though, as we know, it was really nylon), her expensive hand-bag (an old one of Veronica's), her fashionable little hat. She was, without doubt, a 'toff'. They considered her an interloper.

'It's nowt to do wi' you miss,' said a man standing at the

110

back. 'You run along now, and don't meddle wi' what don't concern you.'

'Oh, but you're mistaken, indeed you are!' cried Ella. 'It *does* concern me. And if you think I am not used to houses like this, then you're mistaken about that, too, because I used to live in a colliery village. I know all about condemned houses, and I know, too, that people often go away and leave their animals to starve. The RSPCA inspector told me so. Did I hear you say a cat was shut in there' (she looked up at the dark and decaying house) 'without food?'

'Aye,' said the man, with lowered glance. He was still a bit suspicious of Ella. Her talk about the RSPCA inspector didn't make him less so. He didn't like inspectors prying and asking questions, though at the same time he didn't 'hold with' leaving an animal to starve in a deserted building. Still, the idea of an inspector pushing his nose in, went against the grain.

'Please, *did* you say there was a cat?' persisted Ella, shivering as an icy wind came round the corner of the street and swept into a whirlpool a heap of papers and odds and ends that lay piled up in the middle of the bomb site. 'Do you really mean there's a cat in there?'

The man had vanished, but a woman answered her question.

'That's right, miss. The Simpsons had a cat, and I know for a fact they didn't take her with them. About to have her kittens, she were, so mebbe that accounts for it. They wouldn't want a lot o' kittens in their nice, new house. Over a week since they went, and some of us has seen the poor thing at the window, and heard her mewing. Last few days though, we've not seen her, but we can still hear her mewing.

'Oh, how awful! cried Ella.'We must do something quickly. We've got to get her out. Does anyone know where we can get a ladder?'

'Now don't you go a-breaking in, and a-entering,' said the man at the back who had now returned. 'Get yourself into trouble with the police, you will! Get us all into trouble.'

'But we can't just stand here and do *nothing*!' exclaimed Ella. 'Can we? . . . Can we?' She appealed to the crowd.

There was no answer to her question. The crowd was silent, and in the silence came the sound of a cat's mew – pathetically thin and weak, but unmistakable.

'We must – we *must* do something!' cried Ella again, beside herself. But what indeed could she do? You may wonder why she did not think of the police, who could and would undoubtedly have helped her. But you see, Ella had, for the first ten years of her life, been brought up by Me Mam in fear and trembling of the 'pollis'. The 'pollis' had been made into a real bogy man to the three Sordy children . . .

'If you dunna behave, the pollis'll get yer!' said Me Mam, when Lily and D'reen were naughty . . . 'Give over, Our Lily' (or Our D'reen, as the case might be), 'ha'd yer noise, or I'll send for the pollis and he'll tak yer away!' No wonder Ella thought of policemen as her enemies! No wonder the police station was the last place on earth she thought of going to for help! The inhabitants of this sordid street were much of the same opinion, let it be said. Policemen only came upon the scene when there was trouble – when shops were 'broke into,' or there was a murder. Certainly not when it was a matter of a starving cat!

Suddenly Ella thought of someone who would help her – the friendly RSPCA inspector. She had seen quite a lot of him, since the affair of the swan, and she knew where he lived. Fortunately this would be in his area. He would come to the help of the poor, starving cat, whether it was after hours, or not. In fact, RSPCA inspectors didn't have regular hours, she knew. If called upon, they would always come to the rescue.

It was some distance to the street where the inspector lived, and there wasn't a bus stop, or an underground station near it. When she got there at last, it was ten o'clock, and beginning to snow. She was chilled to the bone, and wet to the skin, but it never entered her head to go home and leave the cat to its fate. Number 197 was at the far end of the street, and by the time Ella got there, she was nearly exhausted. For one thing, it had been a hard rehearsal, and she had only had a cup of tea and a bun since breakfast time. It was all she could do to knock at the door. A small boy opened it.

'A – cat—' she gasped. 'A starving – cat—'

The small boy was intelligent. He took in the situation at once.

'Mum's away for the weekend,' he said, 'an me Dad's out, but if you'll come in, miss, he'll not be long. Leastways, I don't expect he will, but you never know. Depends on how quick he can get the dog out of the drainpipe. He went down it after a rat,' he added, 'the dog, I mean, and got stuck. Me Dad's been there ever since dinner time. Come in, miss.'

He led her into the parlour, again because of the 'fur' coat, but (only being ten years old) he didn't think about her wet clothes. Neither did he think of getting her a cup of hot tea, which he might have done had she been less of a 'toff', and he'd asked her into the kitchen. So Ella sat in the chill, tidy little front parlour, until finally Mr Johnson returned. His face was streaked with mud, his uniform stained. Indeed, he looked as if *he* had been down the drainpipe, as well as the dog, and, as a matter of fact, this wasn't so far from the truth! He took one look at Ella's white face, and drew her into the kitchen.

'Tommy, lad,' he said, 'why didn't you bring the lady in here beside the fire?'

'I thought she belonged to the sitting-room,' said Tommy.

113

'Yes, of course you did,' said Mr Johnson, trying to be fair. 'But it was a pity, all the same. Put the kettle on, there's a good boy . . . Come up to the fire, Miss Rosetti. You look all in.'

Ella had only a vague idea as to how she got back to Carsbroke Place. In a taxi, she thought . . . yes. Mr Johnson had insisted upon taking her home, before going to rescue the cat. Ella submitted, because she knew that Mr Johnson was a man of his word. Before he went to sleep that night, he would find (and feed) the cat. As a matter of fact, after he had seen Ella home, and had eaten a hasty meal, the inspector went out again, found the condemned buildings, and, enlisting the help of the local police, forced an entry into the house. They found the cat in an upstairs room, lying on the floor, too weak to move, and beside her were the dead bodies of her four kittens. It goes to her credit that she never thought of eating them in her extremity, as some cats would have done.

The inspector picked up the animal and took it home with him, where his son Tommy and he nursed it back to life. When his wife came home, she promptly adopted it, and called it 'Ella' after its rescuer. So this was how Ella saved the life of one small, defenceless creature, though by doing so, she very nearly lost her own.

Chapter 9

The Spectre in the House

Ella had a strange night. She couldn't sleep, yet she was not awake. There was something she must do, but she couldn't remember what it was. It was something about a swan in Regent's Park – yes, that was it. She got up, shivering with cold, dressed, and went downstairs to the front door . . . The swan was dying . . . it was shut in a deserted house . . . no, that was a cat . . . *Which* was it that was dying? She couldn't remember . . . she couldn't remember. All this time she was struggling to open the door, but it was far too heavy for her in her present condition, and anyhow, by this time she had again forgotten what it was she had to do . . . How her throat ached and burned! She would get a drink of water . . . She dragged her aching limbs upstairs again and along to the bathroom.

And there they found her next morning, lying on the floor fully dressed, in a wild delirium. As they ministered to her, she raved about swans, and a starving cat, and a grey ballet dress that was lost and couldn't be found. They could make nothing of it. It was plain to be seen, however, that Ella was ill – very ill indeed.

The doctor came, took one look at the flushed, bright-eyed girl, and looked grave. A second doctor came with a uniformed nurse. Finally, a night nurse. The house went about in a shocked silence, on tiptoe. The telephone was taken off its hook, the bell was muffled. A strip of drugget was laid down in the street underneath Ella's window, so that the footsteps of the passers-by shouldn't disturb her.

115

The spectre of double pneumonia stalked through the house. With terrifying swiftness, the crisis approached – the crisis which would decide whether Ella was to live or die.

Wonderful new drugs came to the rescue and fought the enemy. But, in spite of these, the situation was grave. Something was troubling the girl. She kept talking in a breathless, fever-stricken voice, about a grey ballet dress that was lost, and which she must find – must find . . .

The nurses looked at each other. What could she mean? What grey ballet dress? They thought all ballet dresses were white with frills on. In any case, there were hundreds and thousands of them. It was like looking for a needle in a haystack! It was all very well for the doctor to say that the dress must be found or he could not answer for the consequences, but where to look? That was the question . . . Someone thought of Covent Garden. Very well, ring up Covent Garden, and ask them. It couldn't do any harm, anyway.

A dozen ballet dresses of various colours (some of them by a big stretch of imagination might be called grey) were sent over in a taxi to Carsbroke Place, and taken up to Ella's room. She stared at them unseeingly, then, in a moment of clarity, pushed them away.

'No, not those. My *grey* ballet dress,' she moaned. 'It's lost – my lovely dress – the one that Timothy gave me.'

Timothy? Who would that be? One of her partners?

'It's Timothy Roebottom, the vicar's son at Blackheath,' said Patience, who happened, by a stroke of good luck, to be at Ella's bedside. 'He's a dear friend of Ella's. I think he ought to be sent for, Lady Bailey. He might know something about the grey dress.'

'Send for him straight away,' said Lady Bailey, ready to catch at any straw that might save the life of the girl she had come to love most dearly. But it was easier said than done. Blackheath vicarage wasn't on the telephone, and if they

116

sent a telegram, Timothy might not receive it until next day. For all they knew, he might be living in digs in Newcastle. There was no time for delay – every moment was precious. So this was how it came about that the BBC was commissioned to put out an SOS in an effort to save Ella's life . . .

Will Timothy Roebottom, of Blackheath vicarage, Northumberland, please go to Carsbroke Place, London W1, where a friend of his, Ella Rosetti, is lying dangerously ill. Would he please first get in touch with Lady Bailey of the same address. Telephone Regent 269473 . . . I will repeat. Will Timothy Roebottom . . .

Into every house in the country went the urgent call, and it caught up with Timothy taking the choir practice in the village hall.

'Timothy Roebottom – there's an urgent call for you on the wireless,' said a small boy bursting in, his voice shrill with excitement. 'Me Dad says it's fer you, and somebody's dying, and you're to go quick.'

Timothy looked up from his book – he was trying, at the moment, to explain the 'pointing' of the psalms.

'I expect it's Dad they want,' he said. 'Got it wrong, haven't you, sonny?'

'No, I ain't. It said Timothy Roebottom all right, and it was a lass who was dying – a lass called Ella summat. Me Dad says he thinks it's the lass that used to live along of the Sordys in Pit Street, and Me Dad says—'

But Timothy was already up and away, leaving the astonished choir sitting in the church hall. He was back at the vicarage in less time than it takes to count ten . . . He was to ring up Lady Bailey, his mother said. So out he dashed again to the telephone-kiosk at the corner . . . A grey dress? A ballet dress? Why yes, he knew it. Of course he knew it. Hadn't he given it to her? . . . Yes, of course he'd bring it

. . . How soon could he get to London? Right now, you bet! He'd come by the night train . . .

So, while Ella lay, no longer pale but flushed with fever, her great dark eyes bright and unseeing, her delicate hands plucking the sheets – searching for something – something that she had lost and could not find, Timothy was sitting bolt upright in the train (he hadn't been able to get a sleeping-berth, and anyway he didn't feel like sleeping), flying towards her as fast as the Queen of Scots could take him. Above his head, guarded as carefully as an atomic scientist's briefcase, was an old cardboard box containing a crushed grey and white ballet dress. Upon it, and upon the young man who had given it to her in the first place, hung Ella's life.

At a very early hour in the morning, the train drew into King's Cross Station, and Timothy got out. The greater part of the train consisted of sleeping-cars, and these were to be shunted into a siding, so that their occupants could remain in their sleepers until later on in the morning, so there was only a trickle of weary people, those who had spent the night sitting up, walking stiff-legged towards the barrier.

At six o'clock (exactly the same hour that Ella had arrived there, three years ago), Timothy reached Carsbroke Place. He found Number forty-two, and was about to ring the bell, but before he had time to do so, the door was opened by Grayson, lordly no longer, but towsel-haired, grey-faced. The door of the area below was opened too, by the pert maid, red-eyed, her cap awry. It was clear that neither of them had been to bed that night. How could they go to bed and sleep when the 'poor, gentle little thing' was lying upstairs there, probably breathing her last?

But now hope arose in their breasts when they beheld Timothy. This young man might save her. Tall, curly-haired, he looked like a knight errant, thought Jenny who,

118

although she was a pert Cockney, was yet a romantic at heart.

Up the stairs raced Timothy, taking the shallow treads three at a time. Along the corridor he strode, walking softly, as big men so often do, and straight to the bedroom where Ella lay, tossing and moaning in her bed, trying to remember – trying to find something – someone – a grey ballet dress. It's odd how a little thing can worry us when we are ill. You might think that, now Ella was well on the way to success, an old, crushed ballet dress would mean nothing to her. But in her grave illness, she was reliving the agony of those hours in Pit Street, when she had lain in her bed, sandwiched between Lily and D'reen, and cried her heart out (silently, because she daren't make a noise) for the lovely grey and white costume that was not going to be hers.

'Ella, my dear,' said Timothy, a lump coming into his throat as he beheld her, 'I've brought your dress.' Out of the box came the Cinderella costume, and when Ella saw it and beheld Timothy, she smiled.

'Timothy!' she said in a whisper, but quite coherently. 'You've brought my dress. How sweet of you!' Then her eyes closed, and for one terrible moment Timothy thought that Ella had spoken his name and then left him for ever, but the smiling face of the nurse as she bustled forward reassured him. She pointed to the girl's damp forehead, and beckoned him away from the bed.

'She's asleep,' she said. 'Her first real sleep for a long time. The fever had broken. This is the crisis we've been waiting for, and thanks to you she's turned it. You were just in time. She will be all right now.'

Christmas once more, and Ella spent it in bed. The doctors said she must rest for at least six months. No excitement, no exertion, and, of course, no dancing. As soon as she could travel, she must go away for a long holiday – to Switzerland, perhaps, where the mountain air and the sunshine would put some pink into her pale cheeks. For the present, she must spend most of the day in bed, and only get up for an hour or so in the afternoon. Timothy spent Boxing Day with her, and then had to go back to his work. No longer did he have the long university vacations! So she was lonely indeed. The servants at Carsbroke Place talked the matter over among themselves, and decided that Ella was 'threatened' (in other words, that she had contracted the dread disease of tuberculosis).

'Yes, said Mabel Tompson the cook, to Jenny the pert housemaid, 'they always send them as is "threatened" to Switzerland. It shows there's no hope! And so young, too! Ah, well – as the saying goes: "Them as the Lord loves dies young." '

It was unfortunate that Ella, coming down to the kitchen for her mid-afternoon glass of milk, heard the careless words. Although they hadn't mentioned her name, she knew it was her they were talking about – it was obvious, by the way they stopped talking and looked guilty when she appeared. It never occurred to Ella to question what they said, or to wonder if it were true.

'So that's what's the matter with me?' she thought, when she went up to her bedroom after tea. In the mirror, her face looked back at her – hollow-cheeked, paler than ever (no longer a creamy pallor, but transparent, with patches of colour that ebbed and flowed on her high cheek-bones). Under her eyes were dark shadows. Her hands were so thin that when she put them up to her cheeks, the delicate bones showed through the transparent skin. Her beautiful dark, lustrous hair was lank and lifeless.

'Yes, I'm "threatened", said the girl to herself, using the expression that Me Mam had many a time used of one of the neighbours who had been taken to a sanatorium. 'That's why I look like this.'

120

The true facts of the case were merely that she was suffering from the after-effects of a very grave illness; that she was, and always had been, a delicate girl. All this the doctors told Lady Bailey. They added that, if care was taken now, there was no reason why Ella might not become stronger than she had ever been. In fact, this illness might prove to be a blessing in disguise, because it would force her to rest before it was too late.

'A stitch in time,' said the doctors. This was going to be the 'stitch' – a year's rest in Switzerland.

Part Three

Chapter 1

Airborne!

London Airport on a cold, bright January day! Picture to yourself the waiting-rooms crowded with people, many of them, like Ella, seeking the sunshine in Switzerland. But unlike her, most of them were going to the winter sports. Witness the pyramid of expensive, light-weight suitcases, waiting to be weighed before being carried out by the airport staff to the waiting plane. If you could have opened one of them, you would have found its contents identical with that of all the rest – expensive sports wear, consisting of tailored ski-trousers, windproofed jackets, Scottish woollies, chamois gloves lined with wool, wool gloves lined with chamois, gay scarves and pullovers, knitted caps and bonnets. Add to this a second case with skating attire in it – laced-up boots, a skating skirt of brightly coloured felt for the daytime, a glittering one for the night time, when one skated on a rink shining softly in the moonlight like a pool, and lit by fairylamps. And let us not forget our evening clothes, for life is gay up in these little Swiss mountain villages where the rich gather for *le sport*. Every night, there are dances and balls, or festivities of one kind or another. Even the men blossom out into bright colour schemes, high up in the Swiss Alps. (It must be the air!) Oh, what fun! How we are going to enjoy ourselves! What a time we're going to have! Yes, all this was written on their beautifully made-up faces. Only Ella sat silently, drinking a cup of coffee that a solicitous waiter had placed before her on a little table at the order of Lady Bailey, who had come to see her off.

'You'll be met at Basle by Miss Richardson, who's going to look after you while you're at Wengernalp,' Lady Bailey was saying cheerfully. 'You'll find her very nice, I'm sure. She speaks excellent German, and will help you to practise.'

'Yes, Lady Bailey – no, Lady Bailey,' said Ella. Her companion stared at her. Strange how spiritless she had become! She'd always been quiet, of course, but now she hardly seemed to care what became of her, or whether she lived or died. Apart from this apathy, she had made an excellent recovery, so the doctors said. If only she could be made to take an interest in life, she would soon be stronger than she had ever been.

'It will be lovely at Wengernalp,' went on Lady Bailey, more for something to say than anything else, because she'd said it all before when it had been decided to send Ella to Switzerland in the first place. 'It's a charming spot six thousand feet up in the mountains. I went there once with my husband to ski. That was when I was very young, of course – in fact, it was just after we were married. The Silberhorn is a first-class hotel, and you've got a room with a balcony facing south, so you'll get all the sun.'

'Yes, Lady Bailey,' said Ella. 'Thank you very much indeed.'

Lady Bailey sighed. She felt that, although Ella thanked her, it was out of mere duty, and because she was naturally polite. She wasn't thrilled to be going to Switzerland as most people would have been. She just didn't care.

'Then, when you get stronger, you'll like the school we're sending you to in Lausanne. It's not an ordinary school, you know, but what is called a finishing school, and I went there myself. You won't do any real lessons – except, of course, French and German. You'll learn how to make beautiful clothes, and paint china, and play the piano, and you'll go to concerts at the Conservatoire, and plays at the theatre, and you'll be taken by coach to all the beauty-spots. The girls will be about your age – seventeen or eighteen – and they'll mostly be next year's *debutantes*. There will be a lot of English and American girls, and some from the Colonies.'

'Yes, Lady Bailey,' said Ella dutifully . . .

'Will passengers for Basle – Flight number 107 – assemble with their hand-baggage at gate number six to board the plane,' came a supercilious voice over the loud-speaker . . . 'Will passengers for Basle . . .'

And so Ella followed the little crowd of passengers across the windy tarmac to the waiting plane. The luggage was being loaded into the tail. In went the expensive suitcases, the skis, and the skates. In went the climbing equipment of a crowd of young mountaineers, who were out to get experience of snow conditions on the Finsteraarhorn, before their assault on a Himalayan peak later in the year. In went the pleasure seekers, and Ella, who sought not pleasure, but health. The doors were shut, the gangway wheeled to one side. They settled down in their comfortable seats. But not for very long! . . .

'Will passengers please fasten their safety-belts . . . the emergency exits are situated . . . no smoking is permitted until the plane is airborne . . .'

Another reshuffle, as passengers located their safety-belts (most of them were sitting on them!), and regretfully extinguished pipes and cigarettes. Some of the more nervous had a wary look round to see exactly where the emergency exits were – just in case! The air hostess came round with a tray of barley sugar sweets for the squeamish to suck, and a box of little bits of cotton wool for the sensitive to put in their ears. The engines started up, the plane swung round, and taxied slowly across the tarmac into the wind. Then suddenly it throbbed with life. The engines roared, as it raced at tremendous speed down the runway. Like a great bird it rose. They were airborne! The ground fell away, the airport swung beneath them, London lay at their feet like a toy city. Toy vehicles crept across tiny bridges, which spanned a narrow blue satin ribbon that was the Thames. Minute factories, with slender pencils of chimneys, appeared on the outskirts of the city. Below them were mats of green that were parks, threads of black that were trunk roads, a patch-work quilt of sober browns and greens that was ploughed field and woodland, a haze of blue that was the sea! Yes, the English Channel, with the cliffs of Dover looking as if they were cut out of cardboard. Higher they rose, and still higher . . . Now they were in the clouds! Soft mountains of pink and white cotton wool, and islands of whipped cream, floated past. Sometimes, through a hole in them, Ella could see, below her, the straight, poplar-lined roads of France. Then they banked, and climbed still higher, and here there was nothing but clouds, and blue air. For the first time since she had heard those dreadful words in Lady Bailey's kitchen, she smiled. Even her dark secret seemed dark no longer now that she was airborne, close to Heaven, surrounded by rosy clouds.

A dainty lunch was brought round, all arranged on a plastic tray, with hollows for the plates and glasses, just in case it was 'bumpy'. The passengers were lucky on this occasion, how-ever, for the aircraft was so steady they might have been having lunch in the dining-room of a hotel, if it hadn't been for the clouds that kept floating past the windows!

A very few hours after they had left London, they touched down at Mulhausen, near Basle. As the plane lost height, Ella felt a painful pressure on her eardrums, until they seemed like bursting. The man in the seat behind noticed her put her hands up to her head and pointed to the cotton wool that she had dropped long ago. After she had put it in her ears, the pain grew less. In a few seconds, the plane had come to rest, without a jolt. They were in Switzerland! At least, actually just outside the border, for Mulhausen is a French town.

The passengers were taken from the airport in taxis to Basle, and here Ella went to the Hotel Drei Koenige (the Three Kings), where she was to meet Miss Richardson, who proved to be a round-faced girl with rosy cheeks, and a jolly laugh. Lady Bailey had chosen her to look after Ella, partly because she had some nursing experience and was a friend of the Bailey family, but principally because of the jolly laugh. She could speak fluent French and German, since she had lived in Switzerland with her parents for some years, so she soon collected Ella's luggage, and in a very short time they were in a first-class compartment of the Interlaken train.

At first they passed through flat country, lying dead and dull under the wintry sky. Then, suddenly, it began to change. The houses became châlets, the sky lightened, blue mountains capped with snow appeared in the distance, an even bluer lake came into view. A man sitting in the corner seat opposite – a Swiss German – told Ella the names of the places they passed. He had already found out from Olive Richardson that her companion was English and could speak no other language. His own English was excellent, though his pronunciation and his phrasing were sometimes very funny.

'This is Thun,' he told Ella, 'and the lake is called that, too. Behold the fairytale *schloss* (castle)! It is not so romantic as it beholds. No fairy-tale princess weeps within its walls, awaiting her prince. It is merely a museum of the most dull . . . Now we come to Spiez. It is charming, is it not? From here one can take the funicular railway to the summit of the Niesen, and from there see all the mountains of the Bernese Oberland. But if you are going up to the Wengernalp' (he bowed slightly in Olive's direction, since she had given him this information), 'you will be right amongst these glorious

127

mountains. Our next stop is Interlaken, which is the town that lies between the two lakes – Thun and Brienz. I am afraid that we shall not see the big mountains today – only the little ones – for, although it is fine and warm down here, it is misty up there' (he lifted his eyes eloquently to the place where the mountains should be). 'But never mind, *fraulein*, tomorrow you shall see them. Tomorrow the peerless Jungfrau will be framed in your window. It is a sight you will never forget!'

'You know Wengernalp?' said Ella.

The man threw up his hands.

'Do I know Wengernalp? But what a question! Everyone who lives here has climbed (in the railway, I mean) to Wengen, and from there higher up to the Wengernalp. Truly it is a place of great ravishment! Most nice! So many beautiful mountains. The great Jungfrau, herself, will be your constant companion. What more could one ask?' (He grew quite lyrical as he told Ella of the joys in store for her.) 'What a muchness of luck have you!' he added. If Ella had not been feeling so sad, she would have been vastly amused at his funny expressions.

At Interlaken, they had to change to a little mountain train. Their companion took them under his wing (though Olive Richardson was perfectly capable of looking after Ella herself), and found them a carriage. He had taken a fancy to Ella. There was something about her sad little face, her gentleness, her very fragility (in complete contrast to his sturdy Swiss-German constitution) that touched and attracted him. He, himself, was only going as far as Lauterbrunnen, the village at the head of the Lauterbrunnen valley, below the great mountain wall, on a shelf of which is perched Wengen, and above that, Wengernalp.

At Interlaken, the weather had been fine and warm, and the crocuses were coming out in the gardens by the lakeside, and round the Kursaal, but as they entered the gorge of the

Lauterbrunnen valley, they ran into stormy weather. The clouds descended, and black bastions of rock closed in upon them. A roaring mountain river, white as milk, together with the noise of the train, echoed back by the mountain walls and a clap or two of thunder, made it an awesome place, a demon world indeed! Ella grew white, and put her hands up to her ears to shut out some of the noise. Olive Richardson began to look scared, not of the elements, but of Ella's pallor. The Swiss-German reassured her.

'Do not be afraid, *fraulein*. The little one has a touch of claustrophobia. It will pass! Many people there are who cannot stay in this shut-in valley of ours. They feel that the mountains are falling on top of them! See, here we are at Zweilütschinen – the place where the two rivers, the Black and the White Lütschines, join – and it is lighter already.'

Ella looked up. They had come to a tiny station, and people were getting out.

'They are going up to Grindelwald,' said their companion. 'That is the village at the head of the other valley, through which flows the Black (Schwarze) Lütschine. We ourselves continue up this valley, by the side of the *Weisse* Lütschine. It is white because of the boulder clay washed down by the glacier,' he added.

By the time they had reached Lauterbrunnen, Ella had recovered from her attack, but she still couldn't help thinking that Lauterbrunnen was a gloomy village. Wedged in between two mighty mountain walls, each two thousand feet high, it was obvious that the sunlight could never reach it, except in midsummer.

'It is here that I must say *auf wiedersehen*,' said their companion. 'You will now proceed to Wengen by the little train which ascends the mountain side.'

'What? Not up there?' gasped Ella, following his eyes. The rock appeared to her to rise, unbroken, right into the clouds. She couldn't believe he wasn't 'having her on'.

'Yes – up there,' he answered with a smile. 'I agree, it does not from here look possible, but I assure you that it is so. Wengen, as I told you before, is on a broad shelf on top of that mountain wall. Wengernalp is nearly two thousand feet above that, so you have still a long way to go.' Then, seeing the dismay in her eyes, he added: 'But take heart, *fraulein*, do not fear – you will not fall over the edge! And think of it, at Wengernalp you will be right up in the clouds – more than six thousand feet above the level of the sea!' Ella was just thinking that this wasn't much consolation – the clouds looked altogether too grey and wet! – when Olive broke in: 'Why, that's nearly twice as high as Mount Snowdon, Ella, the highest mountain in England. That will show you how high our Swiss mountains are!'

The little train was crammed with holidaymakers, and people going up to Wengen, or higher still, for *le sport*. Slowly but surely, zigzagging along the track, it drew its load up the two thousand feet of rock between Lauterbrunnen and Wengen, sometimes travelling so slowly that you could have got out and walked alongside, sometimes hurtling along quite briskly. Now and then the sound of their voices was drowned by the roar of a waterfall; sometimes they plunged into a dank, dark tunnel, with black walls glistening with moisture. By the time they reached Wengen, it was nearly five o'clock, and almost dark. Very cheerful the little village looked in its mantle of snow, as it appeared out of the gloom! The tiny station was ablaze with light, and thronged with people dressed in the gayest of clothes. There were sledges, pulled by hand, or by big dogs, waiting to take the luggage of the new visitors to their hotels perched upon the sides of the great mountain wall that surrounded the village like an amphitheatre, for there were no cars up here, and, in fact, no road. It was so cheerful that Ella couldn't help wishing they were staying there, and feeling a pang when they drew out of the station, and the lights and laughter were left behind, especially as the clouds had descended, and it was now really snowing fast. There were still a lot of passengers left on the train, for it was going up, not only to the Wengernalp, but to the Kleine Scheidegg, which is a great winter sports centre.

Higher and still higher climbed the game little train, until finally it stopped at a tiny wayside station. This was Wengernalp. All was dark and still. No laughing holidaymakers, no sledges, no lights. In fact, there was no sign of habitation at all, unless you could count the porter, with 'Silberhorn' on his cap, who appeared out of the darkness and seized their luggage. They seemed to be the only passengers who were getting off the train here, for in a moment it gave a funny little hoot, and disappeared into the darkness. No wonder Ella felt depressed!

'Isn't there a village?' she asked in dismay, when the man led them up a rough pathway by the light of his electric torch.

'Village? *Mais non, mademoiselle*,' he answered. 'No village! Only hotel!' Then he caught sight of the girl's dismayed face in the light of his torch, and he added' 'Hotel very nice. You like eet. Tonight all is mist and snow, but tomorrow' (he dropped the cases at his feet on the snowy ground, so that he could throw up his hands in a dramatic gesture), 'tomorrow will be quite beau-ti-ful. You must wait and you shall see!'

Olive Richardson shrugged her shoulders under cover of the darkness. What else could they do under the circumstances? She, too, was wishing they had been staying at Wengen.

Once inside the Silberhorn, however, they felt better. It proved to be a small but charming hotel, and the guests they saw as they were shown up to their rooms, seemed very friendly. They were all delighted about the snow, and assured Ella that tomorrow would be glorious. In fact, this was obviously just what they had been waiting for!

Chapter 2

Wengernalp

Lady Bailey had told Ella about the room she would have at the Silberhorn, with the balcony facing south, that Olive would have a room adjoining, and that they would have a private bathroom. What she had *not* told her was that when she awoke on her first morning, she would be looking out at one of the most magnificent panoramas of mountains in all Europe. Three great giants – the Mönch, the Eiger, and the mighty Jungfrau, peerless in their winter snows, stood framed in her wide window. Ella drew in her breath at the sheer beauty of them. The air was hot and blue, and (she couldn't believe her eyes!) the hall porter was busily engaged in arranging *chaises longues* and little tables with sun-awnings over them, on the terrace that stretched in front of the hotel! Yes, it seemed that you could sit out there in the snow, and get sunburnt into the bargain!

After they had eaten their breakfast, Ella and Olive went outside, and found a giant telescope, through which they could view the mountains at close range, and any animals that happened to be there. The hall porter, whose unlikely name was Wolfgang, obligingly focussed the telescope, and pointed out a herd of chamois to Ella. He also showed her a party of intrepid climbers, high above the Concordia hut where they had spent the night, halfway up the Silberhorn. On the vast snowfield they looked (even through the telescope) like a string of ants!

What a difference there was between the dreariness of last night and the gaiety of this morning! Many of the hotel guests were dressed for skiing, or tobogganing. Some were standing on the station platform, waiting for the morning train from Wengen, which would take them up to Kleine Scheidegg where there would be magnificent sport on the slopes of the Lauberhorn (yes, you could go up in the ski lift), or mighty Tschuggen. Other guests were out on the terrace, lounging in long cane chairs, enjoying the sun, and drinking hot chocolate with half an inch of whipped cream upon the top of it. More energetic people were walking in the newly fallen snow.

Hot blue day succeeded hot blue day. Ella remained in her room most of the time, resting. Her meals were sent up there, and she and Olive had them on the sun-drenched balcony. In the evenings, however, they went down to dinner, and many were the curious glances cast in their direction, as people wondered who the English girls were, especially 'the pale one' who walked so beautifully. It was obvious to everyone that she was no winter sport enthusiast!

Poor Olive cast envious glances at the merrymakers. She was a friendly girl and would dearly have loved to join in some of the fun, but of course she was paid (and paid well – Lady Bailey had seen to that!) to look after Ella and keep her company, so she firmly turned her back on the laughing crowds of skiers and tobogganers. Ella noticed her longing glances, however, and one day (about a month after they had arrived) she suggested that they went up on the train to Scheidegg. Not that she wanted to go, herself, but she was unselfish enough to think of her companion. Despite her dread secret and the shadow it cast over her life, Ella enjoyed the outing. Kleine Scheidegg was a fascinating place. Situated at the top of the pass, it commanded a grandstand view of the three great mountains she could see out of her window. Behind it rose the gentler slopes of the Lauberhorn, a paradise for skiers. And hundreds of skiers there were! In fact, Kleine Scheidegg was nearly as crowded as Piccadilly

Circus in London. People were dressed in every colour of the rainbow. Pink, yellow, sky blue, magenta, and bright red, they sat at the little tables outside the two big hotels, drinking their mid-morning chocolate, and looking like a crowd of exotic butterflies!

On another occasion they went up to the Jungfraujoch, the highest railway station in Europe. On the top, built amidst the eternal snows, its feet resting on a great glacier, stands the Joch Hotel. From its eleven thousand feet, it looks down upon the majestic mountains of the Bernese Oberland. To get up there, they caught the little mountain train to Kleine Scheidegg, then changed to the rack-and-pinion railway, which took them through a tunnel five miles long, cut through the very heart of the Eiger. At stations inside the mountain they alighted, and, from platforms built in the rock face, they looked down at the world far below them. At each stop, the view became more magnificent, the air colder, and, when finally they arrived at the end of their journey, they found themselves in a fairy world of glittering peaks, snow, and ice. They went for a short walk across the snowfield, towards the summit of the Eiger, and on their way they passed a team of *polar hunde* (husky dogs) pulling a sleigh full of visitors. Of course Ella had to make friends with them! She and Olive didn't stay long on the top of the Joch, however, because the high altitude and the rarity of the air made Ella feel light-headed and giddy, but they both agreed that it had been a wonderful experience.

Little by little Ella's strength returned, though it was so gradual that she hardly noticed it herself. Soon she was taking long walks to the various beauty spots that lay all around the Wengernalp.

One morning she awoke to find the hotel quiet and forsaken. All the winter sports visitors had vanished with the snow, and it was spring! The wind had changed overnight, the air had become warm. On the skirts of the receding snow came the flowers. What a carpet of loveliness! The alpine pastures were blue with gentians. The precipices were like gardens filled with lovely alpine flowers.

And then came the butterflies! Of all colours, and in every variety, they took possession of the flowering fields. Ella heard the story of how a famous mountaineer, climbing the fourteen-thousand-foot Finsteraarhorn, had found in that awful region of eternal snow and ice, frail mother o' pearl butterflies just emerging from their chrysalises. What a triumph of mind over matter, she thought!

As the sun grew warmer, the ice began to melt up in the mountains. At night, Ella was often wakened by the roar of the avalanches, as they hurled themselves down the precipices of the Jungfrau. Once, when she was walking by herself in the Biglen Alp – the meadows below the hotel – she saw a great mass of snow and ice thundering down from the Kühlaui glacier, and saw the white smoke of the avalanche as it hurtled down into the Trümletental, the gulf that yawned between her and the lower precipices of the Jungfrau. Although she did not know it, that 'smoke' could have killed her had she been nearer, for it is composed of minute particles of ice that, if breathed into the lungs, causes pneumonia.

Ella would have been very homesick if it hadn't been for all the letters she received. Everyone wrote to her – Timothy, Lady Bailey, Veronica, and, of course, all the ballet students at Carsbroke Place. She even got a sarcastic scrawl from Sebastian! It was Patience, however, who gave her most of the news.

'Dear Ella,' she wrote, 'I expect by now you have quite recovered from your dose of pneumonia. I still remember when I had it as a child, and how they tried to make me drink gallons of milk, laced with cod-liver oil (I still can't look a glass of milk in the face without a shudder), and wear the most horrible, scratchy combinations!

'Everything is much as usual here. The Second Company has done quite a few new ballets, but none of them has been a shattering success. Last week we all went to the *première* of *Le Tricorne*. As you know, Caroline (Rosita) and Angelo danced the main rôles of the Miller and the Miller's Wife, as Guest Artists. My dear, the critics positively raved about Rosita's dancing, and as for Angelo's *farucca* . . .! You should have read some of the things they said about Rosita in the papers afterwards. They took it for granted that she was Spanish; in fact, one journalist made up a whole rigmarole about her early life in an aristocratic Spanish family in Toledo, and how she ran away from her *duenna* one day to dance with the gipsies! You should have seen darling Caroline's face when she read all this! Critics apart, the ballet was an outrageous success, and Rosita was too wonderful for words (or for my poor powers of description!). Warm, passionate, glowing, and supremely beautiful, she filled the stage with her presence, and at Covent Garden that takes some doing, as you know.

'Last holidays (the Easter ones), I dashed home to Northumberland for a day or two to see how they were all getting along. It was lovely to see Mariella, so busy and happy, keeping house for her Robin! Or rather, "castle" would be more correct than "house", because old Mr Charlton (and I say "old" merely in order to distinguish between them, because as a matter of fact Guy's father is only middle-aged) has given them a suite of rooms in Hordon Castle. As you know, Robin had his surgery there in the first place, so it is very convenient. Guy and Jane have the main part, and "old" Mr Charlton lives in the West Tower, which has a glorious view over the Dene. I think it's a very good idea, because these old houses are much too big for modern families to live in nowadays. Mariella says that sometimes they all meet and have a dinner party in the big, square, panelled hall, which is kind of 'neutral ground', and it's great fun. Mariella is as happy as a king with her big, gentle Robin. He takes her home, now and then (to Inveross, I mean), and she says she's getting quite used to being called "Herself"!

'Now I must tell you about something very strange that happened to me when we were on tour a short while ago. You remember, we ended our tour in Paris, dancing at the Opera House? Well, I don't know if anyone has ever told you that I'm half-French myself. Yes, my father met my mother when he was travelling in France, and fell in love with her. He was a widower at the time, and my mother was a dancer. He met her at a party someone gave in Paris. (And, by the way, I expect that's where I get my dancing from.) I've often wondered what made my father marry my mother, because honestly, Ella, they aren't a bit suited to each other. I suppose it was a case of "opposites". Or perhaps my father fell in love with Mother because she had (and still has) rather lovely dark blue eyes with long, thick, black eyelashes, and she with him because of a dashing way he has of holding his head and smiling down at a woman. Really, it's peculiar how many people seem to marry because of things like these! It seems to me, though, that you need an awful lot more than that to make a successful marriage.

'Anyway, when I was a small child, Mother left Father and went back to Paris. I don't blame her, really (Father is so stern that sometimes even I am frightened of him, and I expect poor Mother was, too), but I wish she had taken me with her. I expect she thought I would have a better chance in life if she left me at Dewburn, where there was lots of money and people to look after me, and of course if you only consider material things, I suppose that was true. All the same, I missed her dreadfully (no one can take the place of your mother), and I used to cry myself to sleep because I was afraid of forgetting her!

137

'I don't want you to get the wrong idea of my father. He is what is known as a "good, upright man". He's a church warden, and a Justice of the Peace, and he never tells lies, or owes people money. All these things are wonderful if you are a kind person as well, but my father was never very kind to me. In fact, David and I used to dread his coming home. Fortunately he didn't come very often. I think if it hadn't been for David, I'd have died of loneliness, especially that awful year when I was recovering from pneumonia and couldn't go to school.

'As I grew older, I saw less and less of my father. I thought it was because he hated me, but I realise now that it was because I grew more and more like my mother, and it hurt him to look at me.

'I expect you will be wondering what all this is leading up to. Well, to cut a long story short, while the company was in Paris, I found my mother. She was living in a tiny attic bedsitting-room in an apartment house off the Rue Royale, and she was desperately poor. She had long since stopped dancing at the Opera, and at first she had kept a dancing school, but her health gave way (she had always been delicate), and now she was keeping herself by making theatrical costumes. Although she was very frail, she was such fun! You don't know how much I enjoyed myself during those few weeks, Ella. When the company left Paris, and I had to say goodbye to her, it nearly broke my heart.

'At first I was quite determined to run away from Carsbroke Place (leaving a letter for dear Lady Bailey, and another for my father, telling them what I had done, but not where I was going). Then I thought I owed it to my father to finish my training (although I'm in the Second Company, I still attend some of the classes at school). After all, he has spent a great deal of money on me, keeping me here, and I suppose it was good of him not to stand in my way when I wanted to take up ballet. So I plucked up courage (and I can tell you it took some doing!) and told him quite frankly that, when I was twenty-one, I was going to live with Mother so that I could look after her. I said I would work hard, and try to pay back some of the money I felt I owed him, but he wouldn't hear of it. In fact, to my surprise he was quite human, and he agreed that it wasn't unnatural for a girl to want to live with her own mother, but that I must remember I'm *his* daughter, too. I've never known him be so nice to me! He even said he would make my mother an allowance, and that he would have done so long ago, if he had known where she lived.

'Well, in the end we agreed that I should stay with Sadler's Wells for the present, but that when I came of age, I should join the Paris Opera Ballet, and live over there. I promised to spend my holidays in England, either in London, or at Dewburn. I was glad to agree to this, because of David. I don't know how I should have lived if I hadn't been able to see David. I know he's only my half-brother, but he's very dear to me.

'We thought that, in view of my joining the Paris Opera Ballet later on, I ought to change back to my real name now. You don't know, perhaps, that Patience isn't my real name? It's really Fleur. When I was a child at home, I was so naughty that everyone called me "Patience" out of sarcasm!

'This is a very long letter, but I just had to tell you all about this exciting thing that has happened to me. I don't know how it is, but you seem to invite confidence, Ella!

'With much love and all good wishes,

'Patience.'

Ella and Olive stayed at Wengernalp until late in the spring. They saw the snows depart (although there was always that glittering wall of ice before their windows, for the snow on these mountains is eternal). The cows were brought up from their winter quarters in the valley, and as they grazed over the emerald grass of the alpine pastures, the air was filled with the sweet jangling of their bells (the older the cow, the bigger the bell, Ella discovered!).

Once, she and Olive climbed up to the pass of the Kleine Scheidegg and from there, they travelled down the valley in the rack-and-pinion railway to Grindelwald, the 'valley of glaciers'. Indeed, the cold, green tongue of one of these rivers of ice reaches down nearly to the village church! After they had marvelled at the blue-green fissures and crevasses in the lower glacier, they went up into the mountains in the First chair-lift. As they sat in double chairs slung from a steel cable, and were swung up through the hot blue air, over the flower-spangled meadows, over the roofs of the little *châlets*, over woods, and waterfalls, Ella felt almost happy. She nearly forgot tht she was "threatened". Indeed, it was hard to realise that illness existed in the midst of so much beauty. When they reached the top of the mountain, they found a remote blue lake, nestling at the foot of the lofty Faulhorn, and there, sitting in the flowery grass, they had a picnic tea.

On another fine day, they went to Männlichen, which towers more than seven thousand feet above the sea. At the foot of the actual summit of the Männlichen, there was a little hotel, and some distance away a terrace had been built where one can look down at the village of Wengen, lying a sheer three thousand feet below. Ella shuddered away from it, but she had to admit that it was magnificent

They went back to the hotel, and sat outside in the sun at long wooden tables, drinking cups of delicious hot chocolate. All around them, in a glittering circle, rose the snow mountains. Fortified by the chocolate, they scrambled up to the summit of the Männlichen, and lay on the warm grass, feeling that they were indeed on the top of the world!

Yes, Ella grew stronger every day. The many glasses of

goat's milk she drank, the cups of chocolate, the fresh butter, and the cream filled in the hollows of her cheeks. The strong mountain air tanned her pale skin a beautiful honey colour. Her black hair was no longer lifeless, but once more shone with blue lights. More important still, she no longer felt tired. With Olive, she even climbed the Lauberhorn one day – not a great mountaineering feat, it is true, but quite a scramble, nevertheless – and felt no ill effects, and one day, when they missed the train from Wengen, she walked back home with Olive through the fir woods – two thousand feet of steep mountain path. If it hadn't been for those chance words overheard in Lady Bailey's kitchen . . .

It was now May, and time for Ella and Olive to part, for Ella was to go to school in Lausanne in a week's time. They had grown very fond of each other, these two, and both hated to say goodbye. However, since Olive's parents lived in Berne, they decided that Ella should go there for a visit before she returned to England.

'Goodbye, dear Olive,' Ella said, when they parted on the platform at Berne station. 'Please write to me. I shall be very homesick at first, I expect, and I shall look for letters.' Then the train gathered speed, and she saw Olive's round face (jolly no longer, because of the sadness of parting) disappear in a mist, for there were tears in her own eyes. She felt very lonely all by herself in a strange land.

Chapter 3

Lausanne

There are many finishing schools in Lausanne – over sixty, I'm told – but none of them was better known, or had a more beautiful situation than École Beau Rivage. It was in a suburb called Chamblandes, and it stood on the shores of Lake Geneva (or Lac Léman). The gardens in which it stood were extensive, and were full of beautiful flowering shrubs, as well as palms and magnolias. Ella's bedroom had two windows, one commanding a lovely view of the lake and the mountains; the other (a small, corner one) looked right into the heart of a magnolia tree, bearing exquisite pink blossoms like water lilies. Every night a nightingale sang in this tree so loudly that Ella had to close the casement in order to sleep!

Beau Rivage had its own private bathing beach, and here Ella learned to swim – properly, with not even one toe on the bottom! In fact, a toe would have been quite useless, because, when they bathed, they went far out in the lake in the school boat and dived off the side into the blue water. At first Ella was terrified, but she soon found that it is easier to swim in deep water than in shallow, and she used to float on her back looking up at the snow mountains surrounding Lac Léman – the Dent du Midi, the Rochers de Naye, and the Alpes de Savoie. Most of the other girls could swim like fishes, especially the Australians (of whom there were two), and they used to amuse themselves by swimming under water and popping up in all sorts of unexpected places. Sometimes they swam under the boat, and caught Ella's toes, as she sat dangling her feet over the side!

The school had changed a lot since Lady Bailey's day, and there were not nearly so many English girls in it as there had been then. In fact, there were only six English-speaking girls (that is, three English, one American, and two Australians). All the rest were European, and a rare mixture they were! Ella counted them one day, and found that there were no less than seventeen nationalities in the school! What a noise there was on Sundays, when they were allowed to speak their own languages – it was like the Tower of Babel! The rest of the week, French was the rule.

Madame Celestine Moreau, the proprietress, was a French Swiss, but she had been educated in Paris, and so had 'the accent incomparable' as she put it in the brochures of her school. She was a dark, vivacious woman, as little like an English headmistress as anything you could imagine. She walked about with a cigarette continually between her lips, and was not above wearing carpet-slippers (which made no sound), and listening at doors, and spying upon the girls generally. On the other hand, she saw to it that nothing which could possibly add to her pupils' comfort was lacking in her school. They had beautiful bedrooms (one each), with soft beds, wide windows, and often balconies. The food was plentiful, and as good as (if not better than) a first-class hotel. There was so much cream that Ella could not look at it for years after she had left Beau Rivage. Every week the girls were weighed, for it was a point of honour to send them home heavier than they came! As week succeeded week, Ella saw her weight go up, kilo after kilo. She did not get fat (she took too much exercise for that), but she no longer looked as if a puff of wind would blow her away.

She learned very quickly to speak French, and as for Italian – well, after all, it was her own language, even if she had never spoken it, so no wonder she soon spoke it like a native! She made the most of Sundays, you may be sure, chattering away to Juanita and Maria, the two Italian girls!

Very soon she got so good at languages generally, that she found herself dropping from one to the other without thinking.

Birthdays (*les fêtes*) were red-letter days at Beau Rivage. Usually the girl whose *fête* it was, gave a party, and these were often in fancy dress. There would be a huge, round, flat, birthday cake made at the best *pâtisserie* in Lausanne – a certain Maison Nifenéger. It wouldn't be a bit like an English birthday cake – curranty, with almond icing on the top. The Nifenéger cakes were made of rich sponge, with many layers of chocolate filling, and they had to be eaten with a fork. On the very top there would be a layer of chocolate icing, with the name of the birthday girl scrawled in a contrasting colour. The chef of the Maison Nifenéger was a true artist, and he always insisted upon the girl sending him a specimen of her handwriting, so that the signature was a real one!

When they had finished the cake (which would be after dinner at night), they would dance in the big square hall, with its shining parquet floor, and the ingle-nook, which was big enough for them all to sqeeze into in the evenings when it grew chilly and a log fire lit, and Madame read to them from the French classics – Voltaire, Châteaubriand, Molière, Alexandre Dumas. Sometimes, for a great treat, she would read them one of Colette's novels, leaving out the naughty bits!

Every weekend the pupils of Beau Rivage were taken to beauty spots in the district. Usually they went by coach, but sometimes they boarded one of the little lake steamers, and were taken to places on (or above) the shores of the lake – for instance, to Montreux to see the famous Château Chillon, or to Geneva (Queen of the Léman) to see the old part of the city, and also the beautiful new town, with its broad streets, or to stand on the bridge over the dark blue Rhône from where one can see Mont Blanc, the highest mountain in Europe.

Sometimes they would go up to Glion, or Les Avants, in the funicular railway, and, still higher, to Caux. Here in the spring the pastures are white with narcissi. When Ella arrived at the school, the spring flowers were all finished down by the shores of the lake, but up at Caux, you could still gather armfuls of the sweet-smelling blossoms. She sent a box of them (gathered while still in bud) home to Lady Bailey, and another to Veronica. At night they would travel back on the lake steamer with their scented load, along with a hundred or so other people. It was a fact, you could smell the narcissi from the shore as the steamer passed!

One Saturday, the girls were taken by coach round and round the winding mountain roads to Gruyère, where the cheese with the holes is made, and where a medieval castle stands, its wooden galleries hung with vines. They gazed, shuddering, at the trap door opening on to a moat far below, into which one of the owners of the castle – a former Count Gruyère – flung his mistresses when he had tired of them! On one occasion they went by char-à-banc to the Great St Bernard Pass, and looked down into Italy. Ella felt, with a thrill, that she was beholding her country for the first time!

Chapter 4

Herr Steiner

As Lady Bailey had said, the pupils at Beau Rivage didn't have ordinary lessons. Apart from their French classes, they spent their time learning to play various musical instruments, and visiting art galleries at Lausanne, Geneva, and Berne. They were taken to innumerable concerts at the Conservatoire. They painted china, and baked it in their own oven. They learned to embroider, to make lace, and to do Swiss *filet* work, besides learning to cut out, and make, their own clothes. In the winter, they went skating and skiing up in the mountains above Lausanne, and sometimes (great excitement!) they were towed behind the school car in their *luges*, one behind the other in a long line. In summer, they swam in the lake, went horseback riding, played tennis. Above all, they learned to speak impeccable French from Madame who, as we have said before, had been educated in Paris. Every week, a Parisian hairdresser would visit the school to make what he called *la coiffure*. Each night the girls dressed for dinner with great ceremony, many of them wearing real jewellery and evening dresses designed by famous Paris *couturiers*, for many of them (the Americans, in particular) were the daughters of rich parents. They learned what was called 'deportment', and this means being able to walk and sit down gracefully, not nearly so easy as it sounds! They learned how to sink into a court curtsy, for some of them were due to be presented at the next Court. It was amazing to see how quickly these gauche schoolgirls became chic and self-assured.

146

Beside all these accomplishments, the pupils of Beau Rivage (as might be expected) were taught dancing – both ballroom and ballet – once a week. The instructress for the former was a vivacious Frenchwoman named Mlle Mathilde Renoir. The ballet master who took the ballet classes was Herr Karl Ludovic Steiner. He was a Swiss German from Zürich, but he now lived in Lausanne, and had built up quite a large *école de ballet* in the Rue du Bourg.

Herr Steiner's appearance belied his nationality. His eyes were blue, certainly, but not the pale, cold blue of the German, but dark and deep set, so that when you first met him you thought him a dark-eyed man. His physique was not that of the stocky Swiss either, but more that of the wiry Latin race. He was slender and graceful, with small, expressive hands, and restless feet. His bushy eyebrows met in a line over his highly bridged nose, and gave him a fierce expression, rather like that of an eagle. He was bilingual – that is to say, he spoke French and German equally well. He was not above mixing the two together upon occasions, if, by so doing, he made his meaning more clear! He also spoke tolerably good English with an atrocious accent, and an astonishing use of idioms. As for the other fourteen languages in the school, he could get along very well with them, too, with the use of a little free mime. He used to boast that he could address each girl in her own language, and be understood. He found Russian-born Olga his biggest headache, and his conversations with her were few and far between, and mostly conducted in mime! So far there were no Chinese girls at Beau Rivage, or perhaps Herr Steiner would have truly met his Waterloo!

Herr Steiner's one passion in life was (naturally enough) the ballet. Not only did he teach dancing, but he prided himself on his talents as a choreographer and producer. Every year at the Musical Festival in connection with the Conservatoire, he was asked to arrange an Evening of Ballet at the Théâtre National, the proceeds of which went to charity. So far, each year had surpassed the ones before. Last year he had secured the French ballerina Jeanmaire for his Guest Artist. This year he had even higher aims . . .

When he had heard from Madame that a ballet dancer (yes, from the great Sadler's Wells itself) was coming as a pupil to the school, he was elated. What could he, Karl Ludovic Steiner, not do with a *real* ballerina! She was delicate – she was ill – ah, yes, but that would pass. She would become strong as a horse in this so-beautiful country of Suisse. Then, ah, then, he would choreograph a ballet for her of the most magnificent!

But when he saw Ella – so listless, so utterly unlike his ideas of a radiant ballerina – all his high hopes were dashed to the ground. This girl would not do! He could not believe that she was really a dancer. Madame was making the mock of him! This girl was no spirit of the woods, no sylphide unless indeed it were the wet English woods in a November fog!

He tried to dismiss Ella from his mind, but could not. She was like a sad little ghost, refusing to be banished. For one thing, she was so graceful, her movements so lovely. Why, why, should she be like what one calls in England so express-ively 'a wet weekend'? He determined to find out what was the matter with her. It was nothing physical, he was sure of that. She was the picture of health. But (unfortunately for Herr Steiner and for Ella, too) it was nearing the end of the summer term. The ballet classes stopped, and the school went on vacation.

Chapter 5

Herr Steiner Solves the Mystery

Lady Bailey had made it clear to Madame that Ella was no ordinary pupil who must be chaperoned everywhere she went. Ella was entirely trustworthy, wrote Lady Bailey, and would Madame please allow her complete liberty to come and go as she chose. This may sound strange (and certainly would be, in an English school), but Madame Celestine was so used to strange commands from her exalted pupils' parents, that she made no comment on this one, merely shrugging her shoulders, as if to say: '*Voila, les Anglais!*'

During the term time, Ella did not take advantage of her liberty, but was content to go where the other girls went, and do what they did. But in the long summer vacation, when she remained at school alone, with only Mlle Mathilde (who lived too far away to go home) to keep her company, she went further abroad. For one thing, the deserted classrooms, the beach, where the water sighed among the pebbles, or lapped against the tiny landing-stage whenever a lake steamer passed by and made a 'wash', these places seemed sad and lonely, haunted by the laughing voices of her schoolmates, many of whom she would never see again, since their year at Beau Rivage had ended, and they had gone home for good.

So Ella explored Lausanne and its environs alone, while Mlle Mathilde took her midday siesta, with the Venetian blinds closed against the sun, and a high-flown French novel to keep her company! First there was the modern town, with its shops full of carvings, ivory knick-knacks, lace, embroidery, and souvenirs of all kinds. She discovered an

arcade which housed the top floor of a big shop. The bottom
floor (five stories below) was in the old part of the city. You
could get into a lift (a sort of ever-moving chain of little
boxes) and go up or down from the old to the new, or vice
versa – a great saving of one's legs and breath, for at least five
hundred steps connected the one to the other! She peeped
into the cool depths of the Gothic cathedral, and visited the
Art Gallery. She saw the bridge where Mussolini had stood
and sold newspapers when a boy.

She discovered the funicular up to Le Signal, where the
view was fine – in fact, you could, if the air was clear, see from
end to end of the sixty-mile-long lake. She walked in the Bois
de Sauvebelin, and found in their depths a wooden dance
floor, with a giant musical-box, protected from the winter
snows by a little châlet roof. When you inserted a nickel coin,
music came forth – sweet, old-fashioned Viennese waltzes
(the 'Blue Danube', and 'Tales from the Vienna Woods').
Ella was hard put to it not to dance there, all by herself!

It was late September, and the school had opened again.
There were many new girls, for, as we have said, most of the
old ones had left at the end of the summer term. Ella had
plenty to do, comforting the homesick ones, and showing the
others the ways of the school. She was so busy she almost
forgot her own trouble.

The air was growing colder as winter approached. The
double-framed windows were shut fast (and woe betide the
person who opened one of them!). The central heating was
turned on; huge white pillow-like eiderdowns appeared on
the beds; the girls who were fortunate enough to own fur
coats (and most of them did!) had them taken out of cold
storage. One morning Ella woke to find that the snow had
crept right down the mountain side, and reached Lausanne
itself. All that week it snowed. The trams blossomed out with
snow-ploughs in front, and trucks attached behind to carry

skis and ski-sticks, and sometimes even the skiers themselves when the tram was crowded! Everyone seemed to be able to ski, thought Ella wistfully. Even the babies of two and three glided along the pavements with minute boards strapped to their little boots! Sleighs took the place of the usual line of taxis standing outside the station, and travellers were driven to their hotels with a melodious jangle of bells. Toboggans careered down the hilly streets in a flurry of snow, toppling out their load of laughing schoolboys at the bottom.

Ballet classes began at the school again, and Herr Steiner appeared, bronzed like an Indian after his summer vacation, endowed with new energy, full of his ballet which was to be performed at the end of term. He watched Ella like a cat watching at a mouse-hole. This girl – this maddening girl – looked so full of health, and yet was so lacking in spirit. Once more he vowed to himself that he would get to the root of the trouble.

It must be explained here that, although Herr Steiner had choreographed a ballet for his pupils, he had little time for rehearsals. One lesson a week, only, and what was one lesson in which to rehearse so great a work as that of the ballet of Herr Steiner? Therefore he was forced to leave his ballet mostly in the hands of Mlle Renoir. Mademoiselle had a strong personality, and before very long, poor Herr Steiner's ballet had changed its form so much that little of the original remained. It had now all the *chic* of French musical comedy! Every year it was the same. Herr Steiner would fly into a passion, and Mademoiselle would stalk off in a huff, refusing to have anything more to do with 'that man of the most barbarian' or his 'ballet of the most incredibly stupid'. It would be at this point that Señorita Juanita Alvarez, the Spanish mistress, would come to the rescue. Whereupon the ill-fated ballet would take on a distinctly Spanish flavour. Sooner or later castanets or clicking of the fingers would take the place of *portes de bras*, and stamping of the feet succeed work done *sur les points*! Then it was that Herr Steiner would invade Madame in her *boudoir*, demand extra hours per week for rehearsals, gather the remains of his mutilated ballet jealously back into his own hands, and begin all over again.

This year, however, the pattern was changed a little. There was no Señorita Alvarez, since she had gone home to Madrid at the end of the summer term to be married, and had not yet been replaced.

'So!' thought Herr Steiner, rubbing his hands. 'This is where enters ze Eenglish Miss!'

All went according to plan. Mademoiselle stalked out, and Herr Steiner took over the class himself. He noted Ella's interest in the proceedings, although she tried not to show it. She was not a member of the ballet class, since her work was far too advanced, but during each rehearsal he had watched her steal down the staircase and stand at the back of the hall where the classes were held. His dark eyes, which missed nothing, saw that Ella knew where Yvonne went wrong and that she longed to put her right; saw that she ached to correct Olga's *arabesque;* that she knew that the effect of the succession of tiny *pas de bourrée* at the end of the second scene depended, not on the individual brilliance of single performers, but on the effect as a whole.

'They must be *all togezzer!*' roared Herr Steiner. 'Like ze soldiers, *comprenez?* Like as ze leetle swans in ze ballet *Le Lac des Cygnes.* You 'ave see zis great ballet, yes? Two of you, no? I give up! Zat zere should be two peoples of ze so-called civilised vorld who 'ave not see *Swan Lake* . . .' He shrugged his expressive shoulders, consigning the two unfortunate girls to the Legion of the Lost. 'I say no more. I am dumb – bereft of words!' Whereupon he proceeded to lecture them, non-stop, for twenty minutes upon the beauty of classical ballet in general, and *Swan Lake* in particular.

'And now, he said, when he was forced to stop to draw breath, 'I am bereft of a ballet mistress. *Que faire?* What to

152

do? My beautiful ballet must be laid on ze shelf – So!' He made a motion of tossing it into the fireplace, 'And all because of a dolt of a Frenchwoman think she know more of classical ballet than I, Karl Ludovic Steiner. Ah, well – it is the will of *le bon Dieu*. You may dismiss yourselves!' He waved an arm at the silent, awe-stricken girls. '*Allez-vous-en!*' Then, as Ella passed him, he stopped her. 'Wait you!'

'Me, monsieur?'

'Yes, you. You are *danseuse*, are you not?'

Ella curtsied, as she had been taught to do.

'Herr Steiner?'

'You are not deaf, are you?' demanded the man irritably. 'I asked if you were *danseuse*. I understood from Madame, La Proprietress, that you 'ave once on a time been *danseuse* at Sadler's Wells *en Angleterre*? But per'aps I 'ave been mistake'?' (In truth, he began to think he had!)

'No, monsieur, you are not mistaken,' said Ella. 'It is true that once I danced at Sadler's Wells—'

'Well then! Well then!' cried the temperamental little man. 'Proceed! *Allez!* Go on! Teach them! Into you hands I give my ballet!'

A flush rose to Ella's face.

'But, Herr Steiner,' she faltered. 'I cannot dance—'

'Cannot dance?' echoed the ballet master. (Ah, now he was getting to it!) 'And why not, pray? You 'ave not ze leg broke, hey?'

Elle shook her head sadly. 'Perhaps you do not know, Herr Steiner, that I – I am "threatened".'

'Threatened?' repeated the astonished man. (Never, never had he expected *this* reply. What did she mean? Surely she was not wrong in the head?) 'Threatened?' He looked round the room to see what bogy the child was imagining. 'Who – what – is threatening you?' Thoughts flashed through his head. Military police? Concentration camps? Communist Russia? But this child was *English*!

What, then, did she mean? What did she fear?

'I – I am threatened with TB,' said Ella, flushing again. In Pit Street, to be 'threatened' was something to be ashamed of.

'TB?' repeated Herr Steiner. And now he drew the girl into the sun-lounge and shut the door. His face had grown serious and kind. 'You mean by that, I suppose, tuberculosis?'

She nodded miserably.

'What nonsense is this?' roared Herr Steiner. 'Who told you so wicked and untrue a thing? You were sent here after a serious illness from which you had completely recovered. You were sent in order to escape from the fog and mist of an English winter – that is all. *Nothing more!* My poor child, what have you been imagining? But even if you had been threatened (which you were not), who is to say that you would not recover?'

'They never recover,' said Ella. 'Me Mam says them as is "threatened" is always taken.'

'And who is Me Mam to say such stupid and untrue things?' demanded Herr Steiner wrathfully. 'Why, here in Switzerland we cure hundreds of children each year. If the disease is caught in time it *can be cured*.' He thumped with his fist on a nearby desk so hard that the ink-wells jumped out of their sockets. 'I repeat, *it can be cured*. But in any case this does not apply to you. You have not got, and have never had, tuberculosis. Nor have you been "threatened" as you call it. If you do not believe me, you have only to ask Herr Doktor, who attends the school. I shall ask him to speak to you. You will believe what he says, will you not?'

'Yes, Herr Steiner,' said Ella, half convinced.

'Think you,' went on the ballet master, 'that if you had this disease, or were even threatened by it, that you would be in this school? You would be in a sanatorium, surely, up in the mountains? Your being here is surely enough proof for you – if indeed you need other proof than your appearance. He took her by the arm and drew her to the far side of the room, where a sun-blind drawn across the glass made an effective mirror. 'Behold yourself! Regard the colour in ze cheeks! *Colour,* I say – not a hectic flush. Regard the dimples in ze cheeks, ze rounded arms! . . . If you do not take some exercise – and quickly – you will assuredly grow fat!'

He had said the right thing. Ella's eyes filled with horror

'Fat, monsieur?'

'Yes, *fat,*' repeated the wily Herr Steiner, 'fat as a pig! So get you away and rehearse my dancers, so that you may avoid a so sad fate!

'Please – please, Herr Steiner,' begged Ella, for he had marched to the door. 'Will you promise me– swear to me that what you say is true – that I am not "threatened"?'

He turned back to her and smiled, and she knew that, despite his rugged exterior, his fits of temper, he had a heart of gold.

'I swear it, *ma petite,* although I do not swear as a rule.'

'Swear, then, on everything you hold sacred,' persisted Ella.

'Oh my mother's memory I swear it,' said Herr Steiner, solemnly crossing himself.

Ella gave a great sigh.

'Then I know it is true,' she said.

Chapter 6

The Ballet Class

During the next few weeks, Herr Steiner watched Ella closely – not as regards her health, for he had talked with the school authorities, and he knew that what he had told Ella was the truth. It was her dancing he was concerned with now. Was she good enough – that was the question he asked himself. He watched the strength return to her limbs, as she exercised her muscles, and she was beautiful to watch, but as yet he had not seen her dance. He was content to go slowly – she must not be hurried. At the moment she was merely carrying out his commands, and teaching her fellow pupils his ballet. Instinctively they copied her 'big' *portes de bras*, the pure line of her *arabesque*, her classical *attitudes*. Herr Steiner watched her as she taught, and his heart thrilled to her movements. He knew, now, how good she would be when at last she danced for him.

Ella found, to her delight, that the material she had to work on was by no means 'raw'. Many of these girls had learnt dancing before. Danish Marjike had been in the school of the Danish ballet. French Marcelle had studied with several famous French dancers. Three of the four English girls had learnt ballet also. Two of them had been at provincial dancing schools in Newcastle and Manchester, and the third at the school run in connection with the Ballet Rambert. They were all thrilled to think that they were being taught by a Sadler's Wells dancer, and they worked hard. Every evening, after 'lessons' were over, and before dinner, they gathered in the hall, rolled back the rugs, set up the portable *barre*, and practised for an hour. After dinner, when Madame had finished her reading, they did another hour's rehearsing.

It was at the end of the fourth week that Herr Steiner spoke to Ella again. He had stood, unseen, silently watching the rehearsal of his ballet. '*Bien!*' he murmured to himself. '*Das ist gut!* This girl has even make an improvement on my ballet!'

When the rehearsal ended, and the girls had gone, he turned to Ella.

'Mademoiselle,' he said. 'I have already seen how admirably you can conduct a class of ballet, but now I should like very much to see you dance.' He went over to his piano, and softly played a few bars of the Waltz from *Les Sylphides*, and Ella danced for the first time since her illness. Herr Steiner watched her out of the corner of his eye. A glow had come over her – it was as though she was lit up from within. Herr Steiner gave a sigh of pure joy. He knew it! She was matchless! . . .

When the dance finished, he said without preamble: 'Mademoiselle, I wish you to dance at my Evening of Ballet at the Festival in connection with the Conservatoire. You have heard of it, no doubt? Well then' (as Ella nodded her head), 'it may interest you to know that the proceeds of my Evening of Ballet are to be given this year to the Open Air School for Tubercular Children which is up in the mountains at Les Avants. Although you are not of their number, you will, I feel sure, wish to help them? That is so?'

'Yes, oh, indeed, yes!' cried Ella eagerly.

'To continue,' said Herr Steiner, 'the ballet I propose to present must have for its leading female rôle a girl who is young and dreamy. She must be only half in this world, and the other half in a world of fantasy. She must be in a trance of delight. She must dance as I have seen you dance tonight. *Now* do you understand?' cried Herr Steiner. 'This girl *must be you,* Ella. *You* must dance in this beautiful little ballet which is called *Le Spectre de la Rose.*'

'*Le Spectre?*' echoed Ella. 'But I thought—'

Herr Steiner cut her short.

'You thought that this' – he waved at the *barre*, still standing at the far side of the hall – 'you imagined that this class of schoolgirls were to dance at my Evening? That is not so. My Evening is for professionals only. When you know that the young man who will partner you – who will dance *Le Spectre* – the Spirit of the Rose – is none other than the great dancer Josef Linsk . . .'

'Josef Linsk!' cried Ella in astonishment. 'You really mean that he is coming here?'

'You have heard of him, then?'

'Why, yes – of course I have heard of him. Everyone has!'

'Then perhaps you have heard also of the incomparable Veronica Weston?' went on Herr Steiner, producing one trump card after another. 'It is she who has consented to be our Guest Artist.'

'Veronica!' exclaimed Ella, her eyes shining. 'Why, it was Veronica who made it possible for me to dance in the first place. It was she who paid to have me taught. Veronica who sent me to my dear Lady Bailey. I owe *everything* to Veronica! And is she coming here, and Sebastian too?'

Herr Steiner shrugged his shoulders. The *fräulein* seemed to know intimately the whole of the personnel of the Sadler's Wells Ballet! And he had thought to impress her.

'Herr Scott is to be our Guest Conductor,' he said.

Ella's eyes were shining like stars.

'I can't believe they're really coming,' she said. 'I wonder why they didn't let me know?'

A guilty expression came over the little man's expressive face.

'*Milles pardons, mademoisele!*' he said apologetically. 'I have for you here a letter which arrived by the evening post.

Madame la Directorice has ordered me to give it to you, but your so-beautiful dancing has make me forget! I crave your forgiveness! Since it bears the London post mark, it is no doubt from these friends of yours, and is to tell what you now know from me.'

He sounded a little jealous, thought Ella in amusement. Dear Herr Steiner! He loved to be dramatic – to be the centre of attraction, and she had pricked his nice little balloon by owning to her friendship with his exalted friends. Ella was full of diplomacy, however.

'I don't know Mr Scott *very* well,' she amended. 'I think he scares me a little.'

Herr Steiner puffed himself out.

'Ah, he is temperamental, that one!' he exclaimed. 'But he shall not strike terror into the heart of *ma petite*. I, Karl Ludovic Steiner, shall not allow it!

Chapter 7

A Strange Encounter

Most *artistes* feel the need to be alone sometimes, and, on the afternoon of Herr Steiner's Evening of Ballet, Ella had a sudden longing to be by herself. That morning Veronica and Sebastian had arrived from the airport at Zürich, and she had had lunch with them at their hotel. And what a riotous lunch it had been! Of course, Veronica had to hear all about Ella's year in Switzerland, for, as she said, letters are all very well, but not the same as talking to the person face to face. And Ella had to hear the news of litle Vicki, who was now two and a half years old, and talking a hundred to the dozen, and also all the backstage gossip of Covent Garden and Sadler's Wells, and the latest news of her friends – Mariella, who was busy arranging the Highland Ball to be held at Inveross at Hogmanay, and Jane, who was arranging a matinée of ballet at Hordon Castle in aid of sick animals.

'She's got a positive galaxy of well-known dancers coming to dance at it,' laughed Veronica. 'They ought to make a lot of money for the cause!'

The time had flown, and now it was two o'clock, and Veronica and her husband were going to do some shopping in Lausanne, and then straight on to the theatre 'to find our way about', as Veronica put it. So she – Ella – was free for the afternoon. There was no need for her to go back to Beau Rivage until after the show, for the school had broken up yesterday, although she herself wasn't leaving until the end of the week.

She took the funicular up to the Sauvebelin, and set off for a walk in the snowy woods. Impossible to describe the loveliness of the forest on this perfect winter's day! In spite of the fir trees, it wasn't gloomy. For one thing, there were several *pistes de luges* cut through the woods, and these were crowded with the youth of Lausanne. They threw themselves, face downwards, upon their long sledges, and tore down the slopes. Their shouts of laughter reached Ella faintly, although she could not see them, and the forest paths where she walked were quite deserted. For another thing, the snow had changed the sombre woods into a succession of fairy glades. It lay upon the ground, a spotless carpet of soft white velvet. Through the interlacing branches, patches of deep burning blue sky could be seen. Between the tree trunks, the sun slanted, turning the shadows to purple, and making every twig and frosted blade of grass sparkle as if covered with a thousand diamonds. A herd of roe deer tame with hunger trotted up to Ella, and she fed them with bread that she had brought for the purpose. A robin sang lustily on a snowy bough; the tracks of rabbits and other small wild creatures criss-crossed the rides of the wood. It was all so peaceful! Perhaps because she had been very near to death, Ella felt the beauty of the world on this matchless winter's day all the more poignantly.

She came to her favourite spot in the woods – the clearing where the wooden dancefloor lay. There was no snow on the middle of it, since someone had brushed it clear, but at the sides, the snow had drifted in, making it look more than ever like a forest pool. As Ella stood there, it began to snow. Lightly, silently, the flakes drifted down and settled on her bare head, although above the sky was still deep blue. Ella laughed aloud – it was most theatrical! She could almost hear the haunting music of *Les Patineurs*, and see the Skater in Blue turning his *fouettés* on the frozen lake, with the snowflakes falling around him . . . She advanced to the dancefloor, and turned a few *pirouettes* herself, just for the sheer joy of being alive on such a day!

She walked on and on, and came at last to a precipitous bank, clothed in summer with bracken, shoulder-high, and a carpet of bluebells and primroses underneath. Now, there was nothing to be seen but a scattering of tiny fir trees, sticking out of the snow. All the flowers were fast asleep under their warm winter eiderdown quilt. A slight sound startled her – a strange sound to be heard in such a place, something between a muffled sob and a groan. She looked down, and there, at the foot of the steep slope, lay a motionless figure, face downwards on the snow. It was obviously a boy, or a very young man, and Ella thought that he must have fallen and hurt himself. She scrambled down to him, slipping and sliding, and clutching at the fir trees to stop herself falling headlong. She ran to him—

'*Monsieur! Monsieur! Vous vous trouvez mal?*'

The figure sprang to its feet as if it had been shot, and Ella saw that it was a boy of about seventeen or eighteen. His eyes were wide and frightened – yes, she was sure it was fear. In fact, terror would be a better word for the expression she saw in the dark, slightly slanting eyes of the young man before her. For a brief moment they stood, face to face, then the boy saw that the newcomer was only a girl with gentle dark eyes, and the fear died out of his own.

'*Mademoiselle?*' He made her a stiff little bow.

'Are you hurt?' asked Ella in English. 'I thought you were.'

The boy didn't answer for a moment, then he said in English also: 'No, I am not hurt, *mademoiselle* – not in my body, at least.' He spoke the language quite perfectly, and yet Ella knew that he was not English. For one thing, the clothes he wore had a 'foreign' look. His overcoat was of dark cloth with a black astrakhan collar, and he wore a deep-fitting cap which didn't look English either (although perhaps that was because so few of Ella's English friends wore anything at

162

all on their heads!). He stood holding it in his hands, having whipped it off when she appeared. His hair was black and close-cut, and his complexion olive (unless it was sunburn – she couldn't be sure). His mouth was sensitive, but had an arrogant curve to it.

'I came here to be by myself,' said Ella. 'One feels sometimes that one must be quite alone.'

'Yes, I have felt that also,' said the young man. Then, as the girl made a movement to leave him, he added: 'Do not go, please! I did not mean that I wished you to go. We are strangers, and so we meet – and part. It is good sometimes to talk to a complete stranger.'

Ella stared at him, and thought him very unusual. She might have been frightened of him, had it not been for the bright sunshine, and the far-away, but ever-present, shouts of the sledgers.

'I shall tell you why I came here,' said the boy. Ella, he felt, invited confidences. She would listen, and sympathise, but she would not betray. 'On this day, exactly a year ago, my father died.' By this time they were walking back through the wood, side by side.

'Your father?' Ella's big, dark eyes were full of pity. 'Oh, I'm so sorry! Was it a great shock to you? I mean, was he ill for long, or only for a short time?

'He was not ill at all.'

'Oh, then he had an accident?'

'Yes,' said the boy, 'he had an accident.' He didn't say what sort of an accident, and Ella was too polite to ask.

Presently they came to the dancefloor, and, as they stood there, a man appeared and stood a little way behind them. He was a middle-aged man, with greying hair, and a limp. The boy seemed to know him, for he suddenly turned to him.

'It's all right, Hanz,' he said, 'I am still alive!' He didn't offer to introduce the newcomer to Ella, and the elderly man didn't make any movement to join them, but remained standing just on the outskirts of the clearing.

'Is he a friend of yours?' asked Ella, puzzled.

'Who? Hanz, you mean? Yes – I suppose you might call him a friend,' said the boy. 'A very close friend indeed. In fact, as your English saying goes, he "sticketh closer than a brother"!' Then, seeing Ella's look of astonishment, he laughed. 'I apologise! What I say may seem a little strange to you, but do not let that worry you. I assure you, I am not wrong in my head!'

'Oh, I didn't think you were,' said Ella, although indeed she *had* been thinking that very thing.

'Hanz!' exclaimed her companion suddenly.

'Sir?' said the elderly man.

'I wish you to turn your back, Hanz, because I am about to do a very shocking thing. I am going to dance with this young lady.' Without more ado, he took Ella in his arms, and waltzed her across the open space. Then he stopped, and shouted to the elderly man, who (to Ella's utter astonishment) had obediently turned his back. 'Come, Hanz! I would like a little music.' He waved imperiously at the giant musical box. 'Insert a coin please, and let us have some.'

The long-suffering Hanz obediently produced a coin and immediately the cold, clear air was filled with the opening bars of a gay Viennese waltz.

'Come – let us dance again! said the young man to Ella. 'You are like a fairy! Indeed, but you dance beautifully!'

'I ought to!' said Ella. 'You see I *am* a dancer – professionally, I mean.'

Coin after coin disappeared into the slot of the musical box. 'Poor Hanz will be quite bankrupt,' thought Ella uneasily. Why should *he* go on paying and get none of the fun? She felt like asking him to dance with her, but a glance at the young man's face so close to her own, made her decide against it. She felt, somehow, that he would not like her to dance with Hanz, and (there was no doubt about it) he looked like a young man who always got his own way. Yes, he was a wee bit spoilt, decided Ella, even if he *was* decidedly charming!

All the afternoon the two of them danced together, and not a living soul came near to disturb them. They both enjoyed it, and Ella grew relaxed, and therefore refreshed. She almost forgot about the show in the evening. It was as though she was in another world. At four o'clock the sun began to go down, and the boy intercepted Hanz's tenth coin as it was just about to disappear in the slot.

'Enough, Hanz!' he said imperiously. 'We will now take some refreshment. *Mademoiselle* must be both tired and hungry. Come!' He obviously knew where he was going, and he led the way to a small *bier garten*, a café where they sell not only beer, but all sorts of refreshment. This one was crowded with tobogganers and skiers drinking hot chocolate, and eating sausages. They sat down at a small table which Hanz procured for them by a whispered word in the ear of the proprietor, and Ella's companion ordered a meal with a lordly air, Hanz paying for it, as if it was the natural thing to do. He did not sit at the table with them, but stood a little way off. Neither did he order anything to eat for himself.

Ella felt very conscience-stricken about him. She turned to the young man, who had already started on his fourth sausage.

'What about your friend? Wouldn't he like something to eat too?' she said.

The boy turned and regarded Hanz.

'Perhaps he would. You know, I had not thought of it! . . . Hanz!'

The older man came forward hurriedly.

'Sir?'

'Order a meal for yourself, but do not order too much, or you will be forced to leave some of it uneaten . . . And now,' he turned back to Ella. 'I remember you saying a short time

165

ago, when we were dancing, that the ballet is your profession? Tell me about it.'

So Ella found herself telling the young man all about herself, for after all, as he had said, they were strangers and would never meet again. She told him about Pit Street, and Me Mam, and laughed at the puzzled expression on his face.

'And you really lived there, in all that smoke, and with that dreadful woman, and those two dreadful girls whom you say gave you "what for" if you annoyed them by crying when you were sad. And tell me – what does "what for" mean in English?'

'"What for" meant that Lily and D'reen were terribly angry with me,' laughed Ella.

'I should have had them beaten!' pronounced the boy, with such ferocity in his voice that Ella hurriedly said: 'Oh, they were all right, really. They didn't mean no (I should say *any*) harm.' Then she went on to tell him about the poor abandoned cat in the condemned house, and how she had caught pneumonia, and come to Switzerland to recover. How she had imagined she was "threatened", but had at last regained her health, and now she was actually dancing in Herr Steiner's Evening of Ballet at the Théâtre National – yes, the chief rôle in *Spectre de la Rose*. 'And if you don't mind,' she added, 'I think I had better be going now. I've just realised how late it is, and Herr Steiner will go up in a blue light!'

'Go up in a blue light? *Comment*?' said the boy. 'I have never heard that expression before. Explain it to me, please? What does it mean?'

'It means that I shall be in grave trouble! Herr Steiner will be furious with me,' said Ella.

'So!' exclaimed the young man, and his brows drew together in a frown so that he looked quite ferocious. 'This Herr Steiner is a dangerous and obstinate fellow. He must be dealt with!'

'Oh, he's a darling, really,' said Ella, laughing. 'I was only

166

joking. He thinks the world of me, and I of him.'

The young man's face cleared, and he laughed too.

'If that is so, then we will forgive him,' he said magnanim-
ously, and really, thought Ella, you would have thought he
was dispensing a royal pardon!

They went down in the funicular in a first-class compartment, followed by the silent Hanz in an adjoining third-class
one. At the bottom, the boy announced that he would drive
Ella to the theatre.

'Oh, but I can catch a tram – really I can. It's not far,' Ella
assured him. 'Really, there's no need for you—' He took no
notice of her protests.

'Hanz! My car!'

In a very few moments the car stopped – a long, shining,
black one, driven by a chauffeur, and with a little crown upon
the panels of the door.

'Oh, how sweet!' exclaimed Ella when she saw it. 'It's like
the border taxis in Newcastle, only theirs is a thistle!'

They said goodbye at the stage door. He held out his hand,
and for one moment she thought that he meant her to kiss it,
but on seeing her surprised face, he took her hand in his and
lifted it to his lips.

'Goodbye, little stranger,' he said. 'Although I do not
know your name, I shall not forget our happy afternoon
together.'

Ella was quite sorry to see him go. In spite of his strange
imperious manner, there was something curiously pathetic
about him. For one thing, she had not quite forgotten the fear
that was in his eyes when she had startled him in the wood.
But there was no time for regrets, or anything else. Herr
Steiner was looking for her, she was told, and the great Linsk
was here and was asking for his partner.

Chapter 8

Spectre de la Rose

Lausanne was justly proud of its charming theatre. Small but elegant, it combined old-world taste and dignity with modern comfort. Its plush *fauteuilles* lived up to their name, and really *were* armchairs in which one could lounge at ease; the balustrade in front of the *loges* was wide enough to hold a bouquet, without fear of its falling into the *fauteuils d'orchestre* below. *La grande toilette* was the rule rather than the exception, and the whole effect was one of elegance and grace.

It must be explained here that like most continental theatres, the grand-tier, or dress-circle, was, in the Théâtre National, composed of a succession of *loges*. These were not just a few boxes at the sides of the theatre, where you had to screw your neck round in order to see one half of the stage, but the whole circle itself which was divided up into separate *loges*, and had doors opening on to a corridor which ran along the back. The royal box was right in the centre of these. It was draped with purple velvet, and smothered in white roses, for royalty was to be present tonight – a certain King of Slavonia with his suite. Everyone backstage was 'on edge'; they hadn't bargained for royalty!

'Ah, well,' said Louise, one of the students from Herr Steiner's ballet school, 'it does not really concern us. We are only ze *corps de ballet*. But you, Ella, *chérie* – I would not be in your shoes! You will probably be presented to His Majesty, and have to *baiser la main*. How you say eet *en Anglais?* Kiss ze 'and?'

'One doesn't kiss *men's* hands,' said Ella, as the dresser bent over her with the curling-tongs, coaxing her black hair into shoulder length ringlets, and tying them back with a blue ribbon at the nape of her neck. 'They kiss yours.'

'Not royalty, *ma chère*,' said Julie, another student. 'Foreign royalty, anyhow. The smaller the kingdom, the greater the ceremony! His Majesty will, of a certainty, expect you to kiss his hand, and a fat, oily one it will be, *sans doute*!'

'Oh, no! cried Ella, stepping into the old-world ball dress of palest blue muslin that the dresser held out. It had a much frilled underskirt, a deep flounce round the bottom, and a pale blue ribbon round the waist. At the low neck was a knot of deep red roses. 'Anyway, it won't happen to me. It will be Veronica he will want to see.'

Ella remembered little of the actual performance. She watched Veronica dance the famous Odette *solo* from *Le Lac des Cygnes*, and after that, a lovely little Spanish dance that Angelo had choreographed for her. It was danced on point, but was composed of traditional Spanish steps.

Then came the ballet by Herr Steiner's school, and, after this, act two, scene one, of the ballet *Coppélia*. Ella's ballet, *Le Spectre de la Rose*, was in the second half of the programme, near the end. It is a strange, romantic little ballet that can mean a great deal, or nothing – it all depends upon the dancers. There is a very slight story – in fact, almost none at all. A young girl comes home from her first ball, and falls asleep in her chair, holding in her hand a rose that has been given to her by a young man at the ball. As she sleeps, the spirit of her rose leaps in through the open window, and dances with her. That is all. After the dance, the young girl falls back into her chair again, and in a moment or two she awakes, and wonders if it was all a dream. But no – that cannot be, because on the floor lies the rose. The Spirit of the Rose has stolen some of the young girl's youth, but a sweet womanliness had taken its place. As can be seen, everything depends upon the lightness of the male dancer, and the dreamy, youthful quality of the young girl.

As Herr Steiner watched Ella from the wings, he knew that he had not been mistaken in her. He had watched Karsavina dance this rôle, and, to his mind, Ella gave an interpretation as nearly like that of the great dancer as he had seen, although he knew that Ella could never have seen Karsavina dance – she was too young. As for Linsk – he was in his element, too. His leap through the window was spectacular, and his interpretation of the Spirit of the Rose was delicate, almost feminine, although it would have been quite wrong to call him effeminate. He was neither male nor female – just the spirit of a flower!

As for Ella, during the few moments that she lay in her chair in the centre of the stage, her eyes half closed, waiting for her partner's entrance, she was aware of the stillness of the audience, seen only as a dark mass, with white masks for faces, and the occasional flash of a jewel, as it caught the light from a half open door. She could see the Royal Box, and the white shirts of its occupants gleaming softly in the darkness, and the jewels in the ladies' tiaras flashing as they turned their heads. In the centre of the group, she knew, was His Slavonian Majesty, watching *her*, Ella Sordy of Pit Street (no, let us say Ella Rosetti of Italy – it sounds better!), perhaps admiring her . . .

At the end of the ballet, the audience went wild with delight. Perhaps the enthusiasm of royalty had something to do with it. His Majesty had risen to his feet and was throwing white roses on to the stage at Ella's feet! A bouquet was handed up to her – her very first bouquet! Strangely enough, it was of white roses, too. She held the cool white blossoms against her cheek, and breathed their faint perfume. Then another bouquet was laid at her feet, and another and another, until she was surrounded by flowers. Not even Veronica received more offerings that night than Ella.

At last the curtain fell for the last time, and Ella, still holding the white roses against her face, stepped back into the wings, to be at once surrounded by a crowd of fellow performers.

'How beautiful you were, *chérie*!' This, Josef Linsk. 'I could have gone on dancing with you all the night!' . . . 'Oh, Ella, *quelles belles fleurs! Des roses blanches – comme je les adore! Et regardez la broche, c'est une petite couronne!*' Julie and Louise were admiring her bouquet. Ella looked down at the brooch which fastened a little envelope to the broad white satin ribbon round the flowers. Sure enough, it was a little jewelled crown of delicate workmanship. Inside the envelope was a card which said:

> 'Congratulations from an unnamed, but not
> unknown admirer!'

She could guess who that was – the strange young man! He had been very quick in getting flowers for her. She suspected that poor Hanz had been deputed to do it!

'Well,' Julie was saying, 'when the flowers fade, *ma chère*, you will always have the little brooch to console you! One would almost think they were real – the "diamonds", I mean' (she was examining the brooch minutely). 'It looks quite good!'

It was at this moment that a call boy appeared with a message.

'His Majesty would like to meet Miss Rosetti and her partner.'

'*Je vous l'avais bien dit!*' exclaimed Julie. 'Didn't I tell you so! I knew you would be presented to His Majesty.'

When Ella arrived at the royal box, Veronica and Sebastian were just leaving it. She stepped forward, Josef close behind her, and sank down into a low curtsy, not daring to raise her eyes.

'Your Majesty – Miss Rosetti,' said a voice at her elbow. Then, before Ella's eyes, was stretched out a thin, sunburnt hand. Something about it was familiar, and caught at her heart. She took it, and put her lips to it, and, at the same time, raised her eyes and looked up at its owner. Yes, she knew whom she would see! The moment she saw that sunburnt hand, she knew that her companion of the afternoon had been no less a person than His Majesty of Slavonia!

'Your Majesty!' she whispered.

The young king looked back at her, and not a muscle in his face betrayed the fact that he had ever seen Ella Rosetti in his life before.

'*Enchanté!*', he murmured. 'Your dancing pleased me much, *mademoiselle*.'

Behind him stood the ladies of his court and their escorts, resplendent in low-cut gowns blazing with jewels and gorgeous uniforms. Behind them stood a sombre figure in black. Hanz! thought Ella.

Next day, as might be expected, it was all in the papers.

'All the élite of Lausanne attended the Evening of Ballet in connection with the Music Festival,' it said. 'Herr Karl Ludovic Steiner is once again to be congratulated upon a very fine performance indeed. He was fortunate in having the peerless Veronica Weston, the English prima ballerina, as guest artist, and also Mr Josef Linsk, another very fine dancer, not to mention Sebastian Scott, the famous music conductor who, as most people know, is the husband of Miss Weston. The surprise of the evening, however, was the superlative performance of an almost unknown ballerina, Ella Rosetti. She had not been dancing for some time, owing to illness. Her interpretation of the Young Girl in *Spectre de la Rose* was so light and ethereal that she became a worthy follower of Karsavina, who first created this rôle.

'The ballet performance was watched by royalty in the

172

person of His Majesty King Leopold of Slavonia, who, with his family and suite, filled the royal box. The young king (he is seventeen years old) succeeded to the throne last year on the death of his father, King Stanislav, who, it will be remembered, was assassinated in the streets of Drobnik. Several attempts have been made on the life of young King Leopold already. He was shot by Communist agents as he rode through his capital at his coronation. On another occasion his car was in collision with a lorry on one of the precipitous mountain roads of Slavonia, and he narrowly escaped death. Foul play was suspected. The young king is watched over continually by a bodyguard, and before he entered the theatre last night, detectives searched it from roof to cellars for fear of bombs. None was found, however, and no "incidents" occurred to mar his visit to our National Theatre.

'After the performance, Miss Weston, Mr Scott, Mr Linsk, and Miss Rosetti were presented to His Majesty.'

'Poor boy!' thought Ella, when she had finished reading the account. 'No wonder he looked so frightened when I appeared like that in the wood! I'm glad I danced with him, and gave him one afternoon of happiness at least . . . And now I know who Hanz is!' she added with a smile. 'His bodyguard!'

Chapter 9

Return to the Wells

Ella spent Christmas at Berne with her friend, Olive Richardson. It was fun shopping in the quaint, covered-in streets, crowded with merry shoppers, and buying Swiss Christmas presents. Olive did most of the buying, because Ella made most of her presents herself – she had very little money with which to buy them. Although Lady Bailey had deposited a generous allowance in the bank for Ella's use, the girl tried to use as little of it as possible, for why, she said to herself, should dear Lady Bailey bear not only the expense of her year in Switzerland, but provide her with pocket money as well?

After the New Year, Ella went to Paris, and got a job for a month or two teaching in one of the numerous schools of dancing there. In her spare time, she went to the famous ballet schools, joined in the classes, or had private lessons. These cost her little, for dancers are generous the world over. As a consequence, her technique improved enormously, and she gained in strength and assurance. In the late spring, Ella returned to London. She did not fly, this time, because it was so much cheaper to travel by sea, but she felt as if her feet had wings, and her heart was with the stars! She was returning to the Wells triumphant – full of health and strength, and a better dancer than she had ever been.

Ella's first appearance in a leading rôle at Covent Garden was at a matinée. She danced Odette-Odile. Oscar Deveraux was there, watching her closely. In his article in the Sunday paper he was very kind to her.

174

'Miss Rosetti,' he said, 'who returned to the Wells just recently after a long illness, is without doubt a potential classical ballerina *par excellence*. Her "line" is impeccable, her *batterie* greatly improved, her points are strong as steel, without being hard. Above all, she possesses that indefinable air of authority that marks out a ballerina from a mere soloist. If her Odile does not quite stand out in contrast to her superbly lyrical Odette, we must remember that she is still very young – barely twenty. It is not possible to say yet whether she will merit the title of prima ballerina, but it seems likely that Ella Rosetti will join the galaxy of Sadler's Wells stars – Fonteyn, Weston, Elvin, and the rest . . .'

Me Mam, reading these words out of the Sunday Echo, dried her hands on the dish-cloth and exclaimed: 'My! Who'd a thought it! Our Ella! If it hadna been for our takin' the babby from the Cottage 'Omes . . .'

Lily, with her hair in greasy curls falling over the collar of her artificial satin blouse, nodded solemnly, whilst D'reen turned on the television to *Tell My Story*, and muttered: 'Shut up, will you! I want to hear this. It's Lady Ritson on the panel. Coo! Ain't she a reel smasher!'

'Aye!' said Me Mam again, not thinking of Lady Ritson, but of that small orphaned baby they had taken to keep exactly twenty years ago. 'If it hadna been for us . . .'

At the same moment, in her boudoir at Number forty-two Carsbroke Place, Lady Bailey was wiping the tears out of her short-sighted eyes, and saying much the same thing as she read out Ella's triumph. This was the girl that *she* – Phyllis Bailey – had given to the world. If it hadn't been for her devoted nursing, Ella would surely have died. In the garage at Blackheath Vicarage, Timothy Roebottom was thinking 'Gosh! If I hadn't turned up with that ballet-dress . . .'

But of course they were all wrong, quite wrong! The real hero of the hour was Herr Steiner. It was he who had saved

Ella from herself. 'Of course,' admitted Herr Steiner generously, 'she owed *something* to those other people, no doubt, but nevertheless it was *I* who performed the miracle! If it hadn't been for me – Karl Ludovic Steiner – Ella would never have returned to the Wells.'

Well, it seems that more than one person had a hand in this miracle, so perhaps they were all right!